SONGS OF THE SUNYA

TALES FROM THE SANDS OF TIME

VOLUME I

ADAM H.C. MYRIE

ISBN 978-1-960546-43-2 (paperback)
ISBN 978-1-960546-44-9 (hardcover)
ISBN 978-1-960546-45-6 (digital)

Adam H.C Myrie
word.masons.tablet@gmail.com
ahcmyrie.wordpress.com

Printed in the United States of America

TABLE OF CONTENTS

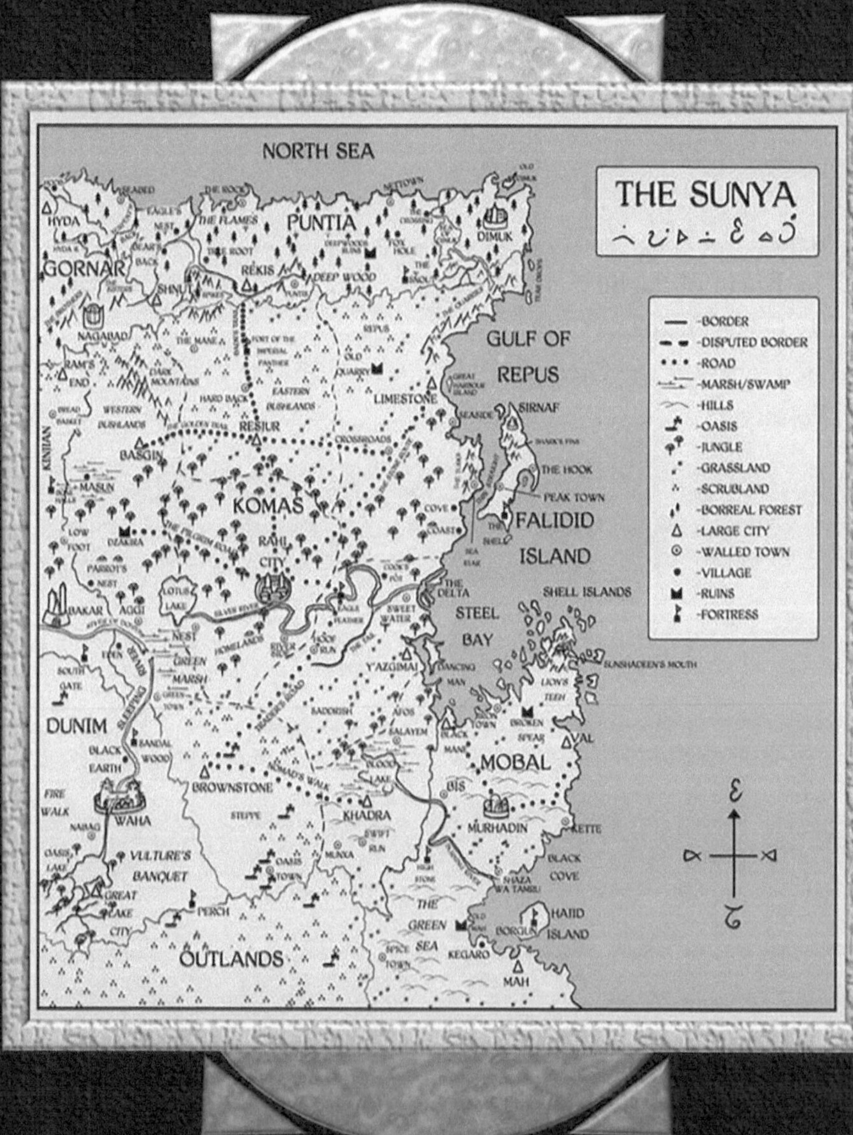

NORTH SEA
THE SUNYA
BEADED
HYDA
THE ROOK
EAGLE'S
NEST
THE FLAMES
PUNTIA
SETTOWN
OLD
DIMUK
GORNAR
HYDA R.
DEATH
BACK
THE ROOT
RÉKIS
DEEPWOODS
RUINS
FOX
HOLE
DIMUK
SHNU
DEEP WOOD
THE
SMOL
NAGABAD
THE MANE
FORT OF THE
IMPERIAL
PANTHER
REPUS
GULF OF
RAM'S
END
DARK
MOUNTAINS
OLD
QUARRY
REPUS
BREAD
BASKET
WESTERN
BUSHLANDS
HARD BACK
EASTERN
BUSHLANDS
LIMESTONE
A GREAT
HARBOUR
ISLAND
SIRNAF
KINHAN
THE GOLDEN TRAIL
RESIUR
CROSSROADS
SEASIDE
SHARK'S FINS
BASGIN
THE HOOK
MASUN
KOMAS
COVE
PEAK TOWN
LOW
FOOT
DZAKRA
RAHL
CITY
FALIDID
ISLAND
PARROT'S
NEST
LOTUS
LAKE
COOK'S
FOX
THE
DELTA
SHELL ISLANDS
BAKAR
AGGI
SILVER RIVER
EAGLE
FEATHER
SWEET
WATER
STEEL
BAY
SUNSHADEEN'S MOUTH
NEST
HOMELANDS
RIVER
SEND
ROOF
RUN
THE EAR
LION'S
TEETH
EVEN
SOUTH
GATE
GREEN
MARSH
Y'AZGIMAI
DANCING
MAN
DUNIM
SLEEPING
GREEN
TOWN
TRADER'S ROAD
VAL
BLACK
EARTH
BANDAL
WOOD
BADORSH
AFOS
TOWN
BROKEN
SPEAR
FIRE
WALK
WAHA
BROWNSTONE
NOMAD'S WALK
SALAYEM
BLOOD
MANI
BLACK
TOWN
MOBAL
NABAG
STEPPE
BLOOD
LAKE
BIS
VULTURE'S
BANQUET
OASIS
TOWN
MUNXA
KHADRA
SWIFT
RUN
MURHADIN
RETTE
OASIS
LAKE
PERCH
HIGH
STONE
N'HAZA
WA TANRU
BLACK
COVE
GREAT
LAKE
CITY
THE
GREEN
SEA
OLD
MANI
HAJID
ISLAND
BORGUN
OUTLANDS
SPICE
TOWN
KEGARO
MAH
-BORDER
-DISPUTED BORDER
-ROAD
-MARSH/SWAMP
-HILLS
-OASIS
-JUNGLE
-GRASSLAND
-SCRUBLAND
-BORREAL FOREST
-LARGE CITY
-WALLED TOWN
-VILLAGE
-RUINS
-FORTRESS

Until the lions have their own historians, the
history of the hunt will always glorify the hunter.

-Chinua Achebe

PREFACE

The Sunya is an ancient place with a history spanning many thousands of years. According to the mythology of the Sunsha, the people of this region, the world was created and is sustained by Sun, who appears in a ball of blazing light that crosses the sky sowing light, life, and favour upon the world. Sun is not a single deity, but a combination of two: Sunshaia and Sunshadeen. Sunshaia is the deity of beauty, love, mercy, and feminine energy. She is depicted as a woman whose body is formed from water. She is faceless, and still beautiful. She weeps for the weak and protects women in child birth. Sunshadeen is the deity of life, war, power, and masculine energy. He is represented by the form of a faceless man engulfed in flames. He is the one that imparts life, also called "divine fire" unto all living things. When death comes, he returns to claim the divine fire of the deceased and return it to the halo of light that wreaths Sun. Sunshaia and Sunshadeen, though worshipped as separate deities are representative of the male and female energy that begets life, and combined they form Sun. It is said that when a man and woman make love, the ecstasy of their climax is the closest they will ever come to being one with the gods before they die.

The Sunsha people are divided into three tribes: The Rahmineen, the Rahisheen, and the Jahisha. During the Age of Innocence they were all one people. They split apart after a dispute between the three patriarchs that gave the tribes their names: Rahmi, Rahi, and Jahi. The dispute was over the punishment for Rahi's great-grandson Izkah, who murdered his twin brother Imsaid over Yahuia, a woman they both loved. Rahmi demanded exile, Rahi begged clemency, and Jahi would settle for no less than an execution. When Izkah was found dead, killed in the night by an unknown murderer, all of the people turned on each other and the patriarchs went their separate ways, taking their kin with them and spreading throughout the Sunya.

The people of the Sunya share their history through songs and poems. Many of these songs come from the years prior to the War of Banishment, when Rahi the Merciful, the founding ruler of Komas and a direct descendant of Bhagir, banished Mauta, the king of the Dzinee[1]. This was the most devastating war in Sunsha history. Forests were laid waste in ravenous fires; many of the mythic beasts that participated in the fighting were wiped from the face of the earth forever, and for the first time in millennia, the Rahisheen and the Jahisha tribes fought together against a common enemy instead of each other, immortalized in the poem *The Axe of Fire*.

Songs and poems about stories like this one are passed down through the generations, memorized by scribes, poets, and elders. They are shared in the sacred houses, around campfires, and at family gatherings. In the early days the Sunsha spoke a language called Old Sunsha, also called the Old Tongue. The script for the language was created during the Age of Clans when the city states began to form and scribes scribbled the first words on strips of vellum and tablets of clay. The poems of their ancient past are more valuable than gold, silver, or pearls to many of the Sunsha. They remind them of the great legacies of their forebears and of the power of their gods. They tell stories of gods and monsters, of heroes and villains, of magic and beasts.

This book contains three stories from those ancient times: *The Ballad of Bhagir, The Great Divide, and The Lioness of the Green Sea*. These stories are foundational to the history and civilization of the Sunsha people, as they each detail moments in history that changed the world forever. Each of these tales has been immortalized in poetic form. They are told and retold, time and time again among the Sunsha people. Now, these tales are shared with you. I hope that you

---

[1] Creatures created during the time of Ama, the first Red Cloak as protectors of the weak, they were born of the corruption of nature and now serve the Dark Sages

enjoy this first journey through the sands of time and into the history of the Sunya as the people themselves share their lore with you.

Salayem na sulayamneen fitayat anuneen[2],

Adam H.C. Myrie

---

[2] Peace and blessings be upon (all of) you

The Ballad of Baghir

Prologue

"Faster! Faster, Grandfather, catch me!" A'azgimai giggled, running as fast as her little brown legs could carry her.

"ROOAAAAR!" Khufu raised his staff high and waddled after her playfully, the polished stones on his necklace swaying from one side to the other. "I'll catch you yet little cub! ROOAAAR!"

A'azgimai hopped over and slid under the bent roots of the titanic trees that shaded the jungle floor, snorting with laughter as her grandfather pretended to snarl like a wild animal.

Sun had just finished painting the morning sky with the bright hues of a new day. Rays of light shone between the leaves of the verdant canopy above them. Birds and monkeys had their usual conversations and exchanged hoots and chirps while dancing from branch to branch.

"You can't catch me! I am the great Bhagir! Fast like a jungle cat!" She stood triumphantly on a large stone, her tiny hands on her hips. "No one can catch me!"

"Fast you are my cub, but never forget, no one is ever too fast to be caught." The old man scanned the thick undergrowth around them with his good eye. "When you are this far away from the village, you never know who is watching, man or beast. Now come down from there, we have water berries to find."

"And honey too, you promised to show me how to get honeycombs. Ama[3] gave me a special egg so I wouldn't lose any." She proudly held up the hollowed shell of an ostrich egg hanging from a strap on her bare shoulder.

"Yes yes, now come down and we can get the water berries, then later I will teach you how to smoke out the bees so they don't bite." Khufu mocked an angry grimace to his granddaughter's delight before holding out his hand.

A'azgimai started to climb down from the high stone when a shape moving in the shadows caught Khufu's eye. There was slight

---

[3] Mother

rustling in the bushes just paces away from where A'azgimai once stood.

"A'azgimai!" Khufu's voice was urgent this time. He quickened his pace to close the distance between them, the uneven ground and gnarled roots obstructing his path. "Come hither, come quickly!"

Before she could answer or quicken her pace, a black form shot forth from the undergrowth, its intent was clear.

"DOWN A'AZGIMAI!" He bellowed. "DOWN LIKE I TAUGHT YOU!"

His little cub did as she was told and dropped to her belly, just as the black form flew over, its attempt to tackle her thwarted. Without further prompting, A'azgimai made for the roots of the tree, crawling under and between them while the beast reoriented himself to give chase.

"CHICHEU[4]!" Khufu raised his staff, now blazing white with the sacred fire of his Ra[5]. *Anu p'at wahdit baq yalla karera laimar! Tag zahit bnit Bhagir dakera![6]*

The panther stopped in his tracks and watched the old man, then looked at the girl. It knew what that fire meant, and the sacred words Khufu spoke carried more weight than his hunger.

"Back into the bush with you! There is plenty of meat for you there!" Khufu ordered the beast. "This cub is not for you!"

Without hesitation the panther returned to the brush from whence it came. As soon as the beast was gone, the divine fire that illuminated Khufu's staff disappeared.

"A'azgimai!" The old man ran to pull his granddaughter out from under the roots by her trembling arm. She sobbed, terrified by the prospect of nearly being eaten. "O, my sweet child. O, my precious little star." He scooped her into his arms and clutched her braided head to the scar in the shape of a panther's claw on his ebony chest. "The panther is gone now. He knows who you are. He will never come for you again, nor shall any of his kind. Sunshadeen will punish him if he does."

---

[4] Panther

[5] The power of an amplified divine fire

[6] You will not take another step! This child is a daughter of Bhagir!

A'azgimai nodded as Khufu wiped the last tears from her cheeks. Her grandfather's heartbeat was reassuring. For all the uncounted monsoons he has lived, his heart was as strong as ever. Sometimes she would lay on his chest, lulled to sleep by the gentle rhythm that danced behind the symbol of their line.

Khufu lifted her chin and kissed her forehead, his scruffy grey locks tumbling about his shoulders. "Let's go home, my precious star; I will take you to get water berries and honeycombs tomorrow."

"No." She replied defiantly. "You said that the panther would never come for me again, and I have you here to protect me, O Wise Elder. Why should we go back to the village now?"

He smiled and put her back on the ground. "Why should we?"

Little A'azgimai stood with arms akimbo and her chest puffed out proudly. "Why should we?"

Khufu chuckled and offered his hand. "You are definitely one of mine."

"I am definitely one of yours." A'azgimai took his hand and walked with him. "Grandfather, when will you teach me Ra?"

"Ra is already within you, my precious star. When you are ready is when you will learn how to harness it. The power runs deep in our family." Khufu replied. "When you have mastered it, you will be able to speak to the panthers like your elders."

Can you tell me the story of the first ancestor to speak to a panther again? I love that story." She looked up at him, her wide brown eyes still looking for reassurance.

"You can ask me a hundred times, and I would tell you the story one hundred and one." Khufu smiled. "Now where do I begin?"

First Blood

(11,000 years before the War of Banishment)

Sun had not yet come up to paint the sky. All the world seemed to slumber, save the bloodthirsty. Silent as stalking cats they sought their quarry. The recompense they came to claim was a long time coming. The brood of Jahi had sent one too many raiding parties, and it was time they got their due. The last time they attacked, the Jahisha took with them many good hides, dried meat, precious stones, children and women: the spoils of war. In truth, the Jahisha attack was reprisal for an attack from the Rahmineen clan, whose attack was a response to an attack by the Jahisha. The feud between the two clans had endured for so many generations, none of the current combatants were alive to see or even remember the insult that was the genesis of their enmity. The only thing that mattered was revenge, an interminable cycle that begat itself anew with each act of sanguineous barbarism. This morning was no different.

"Are we there yet?" Asaburat whispered. "I can't see a damned thing."

"Shut your idiot mouth" Shadiyouni rasped. "You may not see but they will certainly hear your flapping gob."

"Both of you shut up" whispered Rahi. "You are going to spook Wild Cat, this is his first raiding party and I would like for it not to be his last, or mine for that matter. So be quiet."

Bhagir only half listened to his friends' exchange before it was drowned out by the drums of war pounding in his chest. Rahi spoke truth; this was Bhagir's first raiding party, and that fact riddled him with anxiety. Despite being among the most adept hunters in his village, he was no killer of men. Once Bhagir had run down a golden deer and brought it down with his bare hands. The ivory tip if his javelin had broken in the chase. Bhagir had little recourse but to throw himself at his prey and grab him by the hind legs. The golden buck tumbled down and knife in hand, Bhagir finished the deed with the efficiency of an apex predator. His fellow hunters were so impressed that they started to call him "Wild Cat".

When the chiefs of the twelve Rahmineen villages came calling for men to go on a raiding party, Bhagir volunteered. His objective was vengeance for the injury done to his parents during the last dry season. In seasons past, Bhagir's father had done his part in fighting the Jahisha. When he lost almost half of his arm in a Jahisha attack last dry season, he was forced to put his raiding days behind him. Now a man at fifteen, Bhagir was ready to take his place and avenge the insult.

Bhagir's skulking was stopped by a hand to the chest. Shadiyouni tapped Bhagir's shoulder and pointed to the forest canopy with his lips. Sun was painting the sky, and the Jahisha village was in sight. Bhagir scanned the area, looking over the simple fence of dry thorny bushes erected around the perimeter. In the early dawn, there were few signs of life in the village, save the odd mongrel pacing between the conical mud huts, proudly carrying the bones left over from last night's dinner. Bhagir watched the eerie foreshadowing of the aftermath of the impending violence.

The dogs were too engrossed in their attempts to break through to the marrow of the bones they claimed to notice their approach. Y'arit[7] Ayoub, the chief of Bhagir's village, advanced slowly, waving a thick and heavily scarred midnight arm to his chosen men to come forward. They slinked ahead of the band of warriors carrying a heavy log. He pointed to the gate which was an assemblage of sticks tied together with bark cord. The leader of the group nodded and directed his team towards the gate. Y'arit Ayoub motioned to the rest of the men to ready their weapons. Men with shields in the front, men with bows and slings in the back, everyone else stood in the middle and readied themselves for the charge. The men with the log worked themselves into position and awaited their orders.

Y'arit Ayoub counted down from five with his fingers, balling them into a fist one at a time. When he curled his thumb, a battle cry followed. "BLOOOD FIRE!"

Bhagir and the others whooped and roared ferociously as those bearing the great log charged forward and beat down the gate with a single strike. They threw the log to the side and the warriors rushed in. Bhagir was placed in front with the other shield bearers, his small rawhide shield and antler-tipped spear his only protection. As the men raged into the village like an angry black flood, the Jahisha villagers scrambled from their sleeping furs and out of their huts to meet their attackers. There was no contest, for the element of surprise was with the Rahmineen. Frozen with horror and disbelief, Bhagir

____

[7] Chief

witnessed his kin stab, hack, and bludgeon their way through their victims. His spear point remained dry.

"Bhagir!" A familiar voice called him out of his trance.

Bhagir looked to the direction of the voice. There came Asaburat and Rahi dragging one of the Jahisha men by his ruddy arms and matted afro.

"No!" he protested in terror while he kicked his legs before being thrown at Bhagir's feet.

"What is this?" Bhagir asked his friends.

"Do you not recognize the man?" Asaburat yanked the Jahisha's head up by his hair to show his face. "Look at the scar across his nose."

Bhagir looked closer. He did know the man. The memory flashed in his head as clearly as the moment itself. He remembered the scarred man. Bhagir was on his knees, bound by the hands to his sisters and brothers. His mother lay on her stomach, weeping and bleeding from between her legs while his father lay on his stomach with a Jahisha foot holding his head in place, forcing him to watch their crime against his wife's honour. The man with the scarred nose stood over his mother, fixing his loincloth and waving his stone axe over her head. He taunted Bhagir's parents, telling Bhagir's mother that she should be proud to have known the touch of a real man. The scarred man and his comrades laughed while Bhagir's village burned and his father screamed threats of revenge. The laughing stopped, and then the axe came down. Three cuts later Bhagir's father was short half an arm. Bhagir felt the ropes squeeze his wrist. Had more Rahmineen not come from the other villages to save them, Bhagir was sure the scarred man would have cut his father apart, one piece at a time. Now that same man lay before him, a quivering heap of cowardice.

Anger welled up inside of him. Bhagir's wrists still remembered the tightness of the rope that bound them when the Jahisha attacked. He felt it every time he remembered scarred man and what he had done. "You were brave last dry season when you ravaged my mother and took my father's hand. Where is your bravery now?"

The man did not answer.

"ANSWER ME!" Bhagir trembled with anger, his heart pounding in his chest. This was what he came for.

"Here is his axe." Asaburat placed the weapon in his hand.

It was finely made. The stone head was slender and sharp; the leather thong used to fasten it to the smooth, curved haft was discoloured by the blood it had shed in its years of use. A darkness that shall not be named overtook him and with a shout of vengeance satisfied the axe came down. Then it came down again, and again, and again, and then the scarred man was no more.

The Golden Gaze

The moonless air was alive with a chorus sung by the creatures of the night. Bhagir lay awake and stared unblinking into the blackness. He could see no stars as the jungle canopy kept their light from its floor. The last embers from their campfire had died out and all that remained was the smell of smoke and the sound of sobbing whispers. He closed his eyes and covered his ears to block it out, but like the memories of the last dry season, the sobs of women and girls they had captured would not end. Deprived of food and water, their sluggish plodding slowed the pace of the raiding party's return. Women, girls, and young boys too small to hunt or fight were bound with bark cord and leather straps. Some of the participants in the raid where Bhagir got his revenge took turns rewarding themselves between the thighs of their victims. Bhagir did not recognise these men as the kin that shared food with him, were kind to their wives, and generous to their children. He was unaccustomed to the barbarism he witnessed. When raiding parties returned, the women would be turned into captured wives, and the rest would be traded to the other Rahmineen villages for goods, or ransomed back to the Jahisha. The affair was often simple and orderly, bereft of the bloodshed that paid for their capture. If the ransoms went unpaid, the lives of their captives were forfeit. The executions were never done in the village. They were always given to the wilderness for the animals to pick their bones. The Jahisha dead were never granted the dignity of a funeral pyre.

"Shut up!" one of the men in the war party rasped.

Bhagir could not identify the voice, but he could identify the meaning of the rustling followed by the sound of flesh slapping. It sickened him. The image of his mother weeping and bleeding flashed into his mind again. The eyes of the scarred man were burned into his memory. First Bhagir remembered the voracity in his gaze as he smirked while waving his father's severed hand and laughing. That image was replaced with the eyes of the same man on his knees covered in dirt and blood, trembling and begging for his life. He felt for the haft of the axe he used to avenge his parents. There was so much blood. The scarred man's son was watching. Perhaps he would grow up to take revenge on him a few monsoon seasons from now. This was life, a never ending cycle of wrongs repaid with wrongs.

His kinsman finished dishonouring his victim and left her to weep while he went to sleep. Bhagir tried to ignore it, but the sound grated at him until he could bear it no longer. As he rolled over on his stomach to crawl towards the sound, the stars seemed to shine through the trees above and gave him just enough light to avoid rousing those who slept. Nakht was the one that raped the Jahisha woman. He had a wife and three children. He sang the Song of Creation better than any man in the village. Tonight he was an animal. Instead of keeping watch like the chief had ordered, he chose the weakest one, raped her, and then fell asleep. Their captives, however, would not be so rested; woe and terror fuelled their insomnia.

Though the jungle was dark, Bhagir saw enough of their faces to know their fright and desperation. They languished there in agony, bound to each other and the trees. It was another week's walk to his village, and he could not bear another night of this.

"No, no, no, please." She whispered as she heard him approach. "Leave the little one alone, take me, take me and I will give you what you want. Please."

"Fuck him, don't beg." Another one spat. "When my cousin catches wind of what you have done, he will rain poison down upon you."

Bhagir did not answer. He only put a finger over his lips and drew nearer. His heart pounded in his chest as he approached. He saw her trembling. He cut her restraints, and pointing to the jungle whispered.

"Go."

One by one he cut their bonds. The one that cursed him reached for a stone and took a step towards Nakht, but the others stopped her in favour of guiding them home, presumably to burn their dead. Bhagir watched carefully as they disappeared into the blackness. He did not know if what he had done was wise, but he could not have done anything else. His heart would not allow it.

As quietly as he had risen to cut them loose, he returned to his sleeping fur, hoping that slumber would take him. It still eluded him. He felt a presence looming, as if there were eyes cast upon him from the distance. The jungle canopy veiled the stars again and Bhagir waited for either sleep to take him or for Sun to paint the sky.

"Nakht! You idiot!" Y'arit Ayoub kicked the sleeping man back into the waking world. "How could you let them escape?"

"What do you mean?" Nakht squawked, his arms protecting his head from the chief's heavy foot.

"I should fucking kill you!" The chief continued to stomp on the object of his ire. "One of those women was the cousin of a Jahisha chief. We could have ransomed her!" He kicked again.

Bhagir watched as Y'arit Ayoub unloaded his frustration on Nakht, feeling an uneasy sense of relief that everyone assumed the captives escaped on their own. Y'arit Ayoub would surely end his life if he were to discover the truth. Sunshaia would protect him. She is the goddess of mercy, and she protects the merciful, a quality it seemed men had forgotten.

The chief poured water from a gourd over his foot to wash away the bloody evidence of Nakht's punishment. "I hunger. You, Wild Cat! Take up your spear and find me something fat to eat, since you hunt better than you fight. Bring your big-headed friend with you."

The men chuckled.

A respite from their barbarity was welcome. Bhagir's mind was on the edge. He doubted the righteousness of last night's deed, but he would have done it again a thousand times over. He couldn't bear to hear the cries while the women they captured were used again. It reminded him too much of his own mother's cries when the scarred man and his kinsmen made his family watch. Shadiyouni followed him, his bow and arrows in hand.

They left the camp behind and stalked into the bush. The jungle was bountiful. Birds and monkeys hopped from branch to branch in their dozens, and fruit hung fat and low from their trees. The chief, however, did not want meat from the small colourful birds, or the bony monkeys, and he did not ask for fruit. Y'arit Ayoub was not a man to disappoint with meagre fare. He wanted something large like a bush pig or a deer, and he was going to have it.

"Why do you look so sullen?" Shadiyouni asked. "Your face has been sour since you killed that son of a hyena. We won the battle and earned glory for our clan. You should hold your head up with pride. Your father will praise you once you present that axe to him."

Bhagir did not answer.

Shadiyouni raised an eyebrow. "Or maybe it is that you miss Selahst? She is a pretty one. You had best offer her father a dowry before the chief decides he wants another wife."

Bhagir ignored him and continued the hunt.

"Y'arit Ayoub kicked Nakht so hard that his ancestors felt it in Sun's halo." Shadiyouni mocked kicking a downed man in the ribs. "That is what you get for derelict of duty. Could you imagine what he would have done if Nakht let them go on purpose?"

Bhagir sighed and crouched low, his eyes and ears keen to the world around him. Shadiyouni nocked his stone-tipped arrow and followed close behind. The dirt beneath them was still soft from the ebbing floodwaters, and the smell of rotting vegetation was strong.

"Here, mask your scent." Bhagir scooped a handful of wet dirt from beneath the leaves at their feet.

The pair coated their skin with a layer of the strong smelling earth, hiding their scent from the animals they sought. They eventually came upon a small watering hole with trees jutting from beneath the surface like the quills of a porcupine. The monsoon season had just ended, and Sunshaia always left ponds and small watering holes as a gift for both man and beast. She was the mother of them all, and she loved all life dearly. She preserved life, and Sunshadeen was there to claim it when the time had come. This was the way of the world.

They hid beneath the broad hanging leaves of a nearby bush and waited. Occasionally a crocodile would emerge from the water and rest with its toothy mouth wide open, almost waiting for food to fall into it. No one was sure why they did that. Bhagir assumed that it was difficult to sleep under water, so resting on the water's edge only made sense. Their skin was hard and thick. Spears and arrows never did more than hurt them enough to stop attacking. If only a man could make skin like that his own, he would be invincible.

Their patience finally bore fruit, and from the dense forest emerged a mixed heard of golden deer, bush pigs, and a few khurteen[8], storks with beaks so large that they lose their balance and fall when they lean too far to one side. Watching them drink was always entertaining.

"That one." Bhagir whispered, pointing to the deer closest to them and paying the least attention.

Shadiyouni nodded and drew his bow, aiming with one eye. He breathed in and released his fingers with a sigh. No sooner did he loose his arrow than darting forward from the brush came the largest panther they had ever seen, taller at the shoulder than the height of a man grown. This beast was something out of the tales Udrahdu[9] Nabi told around the fire at night. The arrow missed its target, but the panther did not miss his: the same deer that they had hoped to take for their own.

"To the Sunbaka with this, I am gone." Shadiyouni shook his head at the sight of the titanic beast. "We can tell Y'arit Ayoub that there were no deer or pigs. I can peg a few monkeys and we can be back at camp. Maybe later we can try to hunt those women down and bring them back."

I hope you never find them. Bhagir thought to himself as he curled his nose. "Run if you want to, I am going to get that deer from the panther. These big cats are brave when they pounce on you, but they run if you pounce on them."

Shadiyouni looked at the massive panther, still crushing the neck of the struggling deer in his jaws. "That is no normal panther, this was a beast crafted by Sunshaia herself. Sunshadeen put far too

---

[8] A tall stork with a bill so large that it sometimes falls over when it bends down to drink

[9] Wise Elder

much divine fire in this one. I am gone, and if you want to get killed that is on you. I love you, cousin, but this is madness."

With that, Shadiyouni abandoned Bhagir to his fate and disappeared quietly into the foliage.

Bhagir had done this before with normal panthers, though never alone. His father showed him how to scare them off. Stand tall, make noise, and have your spear ready. When all three were done right, the panther would back off long enough to take the meat from the carcass and go. This time, however, Bhagir wanted the whole thing. They mocked him for only killing that one man in the raid. There were murmurs of his cowardice. He needed to prove to himself that he was no coward.

"RAAAAAAAAAAAAA!" He shouted as he pounced from the bush, beating the edge of his shield with the shaft of his spear. "RRRRRRRRAAAAA!"

The giant panther looked at him in confusion and disbelief. He opened his jaws and dropped the now deceased dear and snarled.

"SSSSSSSSSSSS" Bhagir hissed as he stared into the gold eyes burning at him from the midnight stalker.

The beast snarled, then charged, stopping short to avoid contact. Bhagir would not be cowed. It seemed all of the animals that had scattered in the initial attack had returned to watch the spectacle of this slender man facing off with the master of the jungle. Bhagir and the panther circled each other. He kept his spear aloft and his shield forward, eyes unmoving. He darted forward with his spear and feigned an attack, hissing at the panther. Still they circled each other, each testing the other's resolve to win the prize. Bhagir positioned himself over the deer's carcass.

"This is mine! You tried to take it from me but I will have it now!" He shouted to the panther, which continued to grumble at him with ears low. Their gaze remained unbroken.

Bhagir slowly put his spear down and drew the axe from his shield hand. His eye still fixed on the panther; he made a few quick swings and hacked one of the hind legs from the deer.

He threw it to the gargantuan jungle cat, which took it quickly and darted up into the nearest tree that would bear his weight. Sunshadeen is kind to those who are kind to animals.

"You will not go hungry for your efforts."

Bhagir slung the deer over his shoulders; and weapons in hand, made his way back to camp. His kill was a leg short, but the gods would forgive him where Y'arit Ayoub would not. Sunshadeen is kind to those who are kind to animals, and now Bhagir had his own story to tell by the fire.

Poison from the Sky

"Keep your eyes closed, breathe deeply and sink into nothingness." The Wise Elder whispered as he circled Bhagir, a gourd of smoking myrrh in his hand. "The world is void; there is only you, my voice, and the gods."

Bhagir did his best to follow the Udrahdu's instructions. It was difficult, since the raid so many months ago his mind remained uneasy. He was unsure if it was his encounter with the giant panther, or just the memory of the carnage in the Jahisha village. His mother and father sent him to Udrahdu Nabi, the Wise Elder of the village, to return him to his right mind. He often sought the Wise Elder out over the years for advice and to learn more about the history of their people. They would meditate together, repeating exaltations to the gods and seeking a connection with the ancestors. There was a constant disquiet in Bhagir of late, as though a fire had been awakened and demanded to be fed. He never forgot the feeling of being watched that stalked his every step each time he left the village to hunt. Only the village Udrahdu could calm his storm. The Udrahdeen were chosen by the gods and not the people. Sunshadeen would breathe more vigour into their divine fires. It imbued them with strength, wisdom, and the power to communicate with nature. The people called it their Ra, which manifested itself in a smokeless white fire that swathed their bodies when called upon. It is said that among the Udrahdeen that are also warriors, their weapons glow white hot with the strength of their divine fire. Bhagir had seen Udrahdu Nabi's power. He healed wounds, lit fires, and breathed life into stillborn babes. Now Bhagir came to him to seek healing for his troubled mind.

Nabi was the oldest man in the village. It has been said that he had seen over one hundred monsoons. His locks were long, natty, and almost as white as sun-bleached bone. The precious stones around his neck clacked together as he paced back and forth bent-backed on the dirt floor in the sacred hut. He muttered prayers to the gods and requested divine favour for Bhagir, who had always been devoted to their service.

"You are still, but you are not in stillness, young Bhagir." The old shaman blew more plumes of smoke over Bhagir, adding to the already thick haze of perfumed air. "I can sense that your mind is running from something. What are you running from? Do not say, but answer in your mind and face it. This life is not easy, and these times are troubled. Know that you are not alone."

Bhagir's mind was running. It would not stop. Were it not for Shadiyouni's testimony, no one would have believed Bhagir's story about the panther. Y'arit Ayoub assumed that he had taken a half-eaten carcass and was ready to flog Bhagir for bringing old meat. When he saw that it was fresh, and Shadiyouni spoke up on his behalf, the chief stayed his hand.

The burning golden eyes of that great panther seared their way into his mind and refused to leave. Every time Bhagir closed his eyes, they were there, staring into his divine fire.

"I saw something in the jungle, O Udrahdu. It was a great panther; his eyes were like golden fire. Every time I close my eyes I see them staring into me. He was no common jungle cat." Bhagir hung his head, sitting with his legs crossed. "What was he?"

"So you finally ask me about him. It took you long enough, young Wild Cat." Udrahdu Nabi smiled. "You have met Tikursene, the guardian of the jungle. His was the meat you took. He stalks the jungle and protects the balance of nature. You are fortunate; few men have ever met him and survived."

Bhagir opened his eyes and lifted his head. "Then how did you know about him? How did you know what I saw without me telling you?"

"I am as old as I am for a reason young Bhagir. Don't ask questions you can't handle answers for just yet." Udrahdu Nabi placed the gourd down and sat across from Bhagir. "When the gods saw that our kind had become so cruel to nature and ourselves, Sunshaia fashioned this guardian to protect the balance she and Sunshadeen created. He cares little for the cruelty we do to each other. It is the natural order he protects. He watches for the good we do, and punishes us for the evils we commit against what the gods have given us."

"Then why did he not kill me, and why did he let me take the meat?" Bhagir was confused.

Udrahdu Nabi smiled, but did not answer.

"O Udrahdu, why?" Bhagir asked again.

"He saw something in you it seems. He shows himself to a select few. When he revealed himself to you, you showed your quality when you shared the meat with him." Nabi added another pinch of incense to the gourd. "You faced him without fear, and even when you thought you had triumphed, you were generous in your victory. He could have broken you in half, but you gave him a reason not to."

"Thank you, O Udrahdu." Bhagir bowed his head before getting up to leave. "I wish that I could stay, but I am certain that my father has work for me to do. Three hands are better than one."

The Wise Elder chuckled. "I want you to think about what I have told you. You have shown your quality to the gods. They are watching you now. Give my regards to Aderfi and Kahina. Tell your mother that I am looking for another cup of roast fish and honey."

"I will; thank you." Bhagir bowed again before backing out. It was rude to show one's back to the Udrahdu when leaving his hut, and Bhagir had nothing but respect for Nabi.

It was he that pulled him out of his mother when the dulit[10] could not turn him back the right way in his mother's womb when he broke water.

Sun smiled upon the Sunya that day. The day was bright and temperate. Sun's heat felt like a pair of comforting hands on his shoulders. Women walked back and forth with jugs of water or bundles of fruit on their heads, men smoked forest herbs in their gourd pipes while they made or repaired tools, and children ran to

---

[10] Women with the special skill of aiding in childbirth

and fro, fighting mock battles with their sticks. If only they knew the true horror of the fights they mimicked.

Bhagir passed between the mud and thatch huts, his mind still in the jungle with Tikursene. He wanted to see him again, but the prospect terrified him. If what Udrahdu Nabi said was true, then the next encounter with nature's guardian may not be so cordial.

"Bhagir!" The voice that called him was honey to his ear.

He smiled and turned to the direction of music that called his name. "Selahst."

There she stood, flawless mahogany skin bathed in celestial light. Her eyes were the night, for dark as they were, they gleamed with the light of a thousand times a thousand stars. The smile with which she greeted him was an ivory half-moon shining from betwixt her full lips. Selahst was the most beautiful woman he had ever seen. She was yet promised to no one, and was an apprentice to her mother, A'azgimai, the local dulit.

"How was it?" She asked.

Bhagir could not answer. His tongue was heavy in his mouth.

"Bhagir, how was it?" She stepped closer to him, and his heart fluttered.

"How was what?" His mind was blank.

"The visit with Udrahdu Nabi you khurt!" She always called him that when she thought he was being awkward.

"It went well." Bhagir replied. "The usual ancient wisdom, um, things, gods, um…wisdom."

"I am glad to hear that he has been helping you." She replied, adjusting the jug of water resting on her braids. "I always hear that the first raid is always the hardest. If you ever need to talk, you know where to find me." There was that half-moon again.

"Th-thank you." Bhagir nodded.

"I have to go now, it's almost time to start making supper. May the gods sow favour on you."

Bhagir waved awkwardly as she continued on to her parents' hut. She was always so kind to him. She understood the softness of his nature and unlike many of the others in the village; Selahst offered him a kind ear. While his parents recovered from the Jahisha attack in the last dry season, her mother and father sent her to his family to bring food and help his sisters tend the home. Bhagir wanted to marry her, but he had yet to prove his worth to her father. After seeing his lack of ferocity in the raiding party, it was unlikely that Bhagir would ever be considered an acceptable suitor for Selahst, but one could only dream.

Upon returning to his parents' hut, he greeted them with a kiss on the hand and passed on the Udrahdu's regards. His mother smiled at the request for honeyed fish. She chucked and mused about Udrahdu Nabi's constant attempts to get a cup of her food in his hands. He would always put his special herbs in it and consume it like it was an elixir of immortality, then chided Bhagir's father and siblings about how little they appreciated her and the food she prepared. This was a claim that his father and his brothers protested with great smiles on their faces.

"How was your visit with the Udrahdu?" Bhagir's father asked.

"It went well. I feel better each time I see him." Bhagir replied.

"Good." His mother replied. "We need firewood for your sisters and me to cook supper. Go with your father and brothers."

His mother continued to provide Bhagir with a list of chores she had in mind for him. Tanning a deer hide given to them by a neighbour, helping his father rethatch the roof while dinner was being cooked, helping his father make a new spear, and the list went on. Bhagir closed his eyes and saw those burning golden eyes again, this time, they watched from the other side of the thorn bush barrier they had erected around their village to keep the Jahisha and other wild animals out. Hot breath blew over the back of his neck and a voice whispered.

"Run."

Bhagir opened his eyes to the sound of shouting. He and his family ran outside to see the cause of the commotion. Someone was throwing clay pots full of cobras and scorpions from the jungle. The pots shattered as they hit the ground, releasing dozens upon dozens of the venomous creatures into the village. There was running and screaming. Women lifted up their children and ran into or out of their homes. Many were bitten in the chaos. They would not survive.

Udrahdu Nabi emerged from the sacred hut and raised his hand. "Peace and be still!"

His staff burned white with the power of his Ra. He muttered some words of prayer and touched his staff to the ground. The cobras and scorpions stopped in their tracks, turned, and made their way out of the village and into the jungle.

Y'arit Ayoub stormed out of his hut, weapons in hand. He beat his meaty his chest with an angry fist and shouted. "Gather your weapons! They are out there and we will find them."

No further words were needed. Every man strong enough to fight grabbed the nearest implement of death at hand and rushed out of the open gate into the wilderness. Blood would run in the jungle this day.

Bhagir's father took up the axe that took his hand. "Get your spear and shield son, we have Jahisha to kill. Tikurgimai, Balamuzkat, stay with your mother and sisters. Kahina, Bhagir and I will be back shortly."

Bhagir's mother kissed her husband's lips "May the Sunshadeen give you strength, Aderfi. Bhagir, stay close to your father. Both of you, come back to me."

Bhagir did as he was told and with his father followed the ravenous war party into the bush. There was no formation and no plan. They simply ran out among the trees to meet their foes, ready to draw blood. Occasionally they changed direction in response to shouts of "Over there!" and "Behind those trees!" Their attackers had disappeared like ghosts into the verdant foliage.

Y'arit Ayoub called for them to halt. "Where are they?" He panted; his back sweaty from the chase.

"I don't see anyone. Perhaps we should return." Shouted Asaburat.

"What is that over there?" Said another.

The men of the war party all turned their eyes in the direction of a Jahisha man covered in mud and holding something in a large leaf bundle. Before the first arrow or stone could fly, he flung it with all of his might towards them. The bundle exploded at their feet into a swarm of furious bees; then the stinging began. Some of the men's faces swelled into unnatural shapes as they desperately gasped for air and expired. The rest tucked tail and scattered in all directions.

"RUN TO THE OTHER VILLAGES! TELL THEM WE ARE UNDER ATTACK!" Y'arit Ayoub shouted.

No one heeded his order. The bees were too many, too loud, and the stings too painful. Bhagir grabbed his father by the forearm and the pair ran in the direction of the nearest watering hole. If there was water, there was mud. They could hide in the water or cover their skin with mud to protect them from the stings. The speed of their pace did not matter; the bees were faster, though with every step, more of them seemed to lose interest. The number of stings made their skins tender and their bodies weak. They came to a small pond and collapsed in the wet clay of its edge, gasping for air. The bees abandoned the chase, but another pursuer was watching.

"Are you alright, son?" Aderfi asked. "Let me see your back." Aderfi inspected his son's skin and clicked his tongue. "Those Jahisha bastards, they will be repaid in kind."

He tore some of the thick bark from the nearest tree and began to scrape at Bhagir's skin to remove the stingers. Bhagir winced as he felt each one tear out of his flesh. His father's hand was gentle and swift. Before long most of the stingers were gone from his flesh. Bhagir took the bark and began to do the same for his father, and then they were interrupted.

A group of men in war paint came screaming from the bushes, their war clubs, spears, and axes in hand. Bhagir and his father took up their arms and prepared to fight. This was no timeto hesitate. Though he only had one arm, Aderfi was fast with the axe and used the stump at the end of his arm to couch the blows as they came. He was a warrior at heart, more fighter than hunter. He slipped blows, caught arms, hacked at knees, and kicked his opponents between their legs. In the blink of an eye he had already killed three men, leaving the others to keep a cautious distance from his reach.

Two of the attackers barrelled forward at Bhagir. He caught the blow from one assailant's war club with his shield and drove the other back with the point of his spear. He pulled the spear back and using the blunt end struck man at his shield, checked him back again with his shoulder and ran him through with the spear. He met the man's eyes as he took the thrust. His mouth bled and his body shuddered. Bhagir felt it down the shaft of his weapon. He let go of his spear and took up the war club of his fallen foe, prepared to meet the other man returning for a second attack. More men spilled out of the jungle with murder in their eyes. Bhagir picked up his feet and sprinted to his father's side. They stood back to back, facing their assailants. Bhagir's skin was hot and wet with streams of sweat stinging his body where the bees had bitten him.

"Father, if I have offended you in any way in my whole life, I beg your forgiveness." Bhagir panted.

"Bhagir, I want you to run." Aderfi said. "I need you to run."

Before Bhagir could respond the attack came again. A stone axe swung for Bhagir's head. He ducked and responded with the head of his club across the temple of the assailant, killing him instantly. A spear thrust came for his belly. His shield caught the blow, and the barbed ivory head caught itself in the rawhide. When the spearman drew backward, the shield was ripped from Bhagir's hand. He stooped down to pick up the dropped axe when another spear thrust meant for his chest passed over him and stuck his father in the back. Aderfi gasped as the weapon was pressed forward by its bearer. Bhagir shouted with rage and with a cry of blood fire, he threw himself forward and split the top of the spearman's head open with one strike of the axe. His war club was thirsty as well, and drank from the broken skull of another Jahisha that came for him.

"Bhagir! RUN!" His father shouted from his knees, the spear still protruding from his blood soaked back while he continued to swing his weapon.

Bhagir obeyed and through the gap created by the men he killed, he darted off looking for cover in the undergrowth. They did not chase him, for his father, though wounded, fought them to his last, shouting for Bhagir to run as he cut them down as best he could. Bhagir ran until the shouting stopped. He knew that Sunshadeen had come to collect Aderfi's divine fire, and what a fire it was. He looked at the weapons in his hands, they were bloody. His hands were bloody. His chest was bloody. He knew that the Jahisha would enter the village once all the men were dead or scattered. They needed help. He resolved to run to the nearest village and beg the chief to call up a war party.

He ran again, as fast as his legs would carry him. He ducked under branches, charged through walls of leaves and leaped over stones and gnarled roots. He took a sharp turn around an especially thick tree trunk and came face to face with a snarling panther. This one was normal sized, and did not look interested in testing Bhagir's quality. The panther growled at him and pounced. As his father taught him, Bhagir threw himself down and rolled towards the cat, passing under him and avoiding the attack entirely. He raised his weapons and prepared to fight for his life again. The jungle cat prodded at Bhagir, testing the young warrior with tentative swipes of his knife-sharp claws. Bhagir breathed slowly, looking the panther in the eyes and keeping the war club ahead of him and his axe high and ready to strike. Something caught the corner of his eye. A slender shape slowly rose from a pile of leaves behind the panther and expanded its hood. The cobra looked at both of them with cold eyes and struck. The panther jumped and yowled in pain and turned around to bat down the serpent's head before decapitating it entirely with his jaws.

The panther returned his attention to Bhagir, high on the blood of the serpent he just killed. The jungle cat advanced two steps, and then collapsed, convulsing and writhing in pain. Bhagir shook his head, thanked his good fortune, and then turned to run. The cobra had saved him by biting the panther that intended to kill him. The gods were merciful.

As he came nearer to the village of his kinsmen, he heard a familiar grumble in the bush. He stopped running and listened, his chest heaving from exhaustion. He felt the hot breath on the back of his neck again, and turned to see who it was. The growling persisted, and the hot breathing on his neck continued.

"Tikursene, I know you are here." He called out. "Show yourself."

Bhagir turned again and saw the great panther, eyes of golden fire fixed upon him.

"If you have come to kill me then kill me." Bhagir thought of his father and the tears began to flow. "If you have come to kill me, THEN KILL ME!"

Tikursene stood there watching him and did nothing.

"What do you want?"

"Panther" a voice whispered in Bhagir's head. "Panther."

Tikursene turned his back and melted into the jungle.

Bhagir knew what to do. He sprinted back to where the panther had been bitten; there the creature lay motionless on the jungle floor. He prodded at the beast to check for signs of life. The panther lifted his head and growled feebly, making a weak attempt at scratching him. There was no strength left in him. Bhagir knew who could help. Udrahdit Ru'a, the elder of the village Bhagir was running to, possessed the power to heal this cat, she was his great grandmother and she loved him. She would give to him anything that he asked if she could grant it. Against his better judgement, Bhagir dropped the war club and slung the panther over his shoulders. Sunshadeen is kind to those who are kind to animals; hopefully, he would be kind to Bhagir and change the panther's mind about killing him. The village of his kinfolk was not far, perhaps there would be still be time to save his own.

<u>Divine Fire</u>

She rocked back and forth over the dying panther, blowing sacred smoke over his body and asking Sunshadeen to give him strength. Bhagir sat in the corner of his great grandmother's sacred hut, axe in hand, prepared for an unwelcome surprise from his new charge. From the moment he brought the panther in on his shoulders, she knew why he was there and what needed to be done. His great grandmother always knew. Udrahdit Ru'a just knew.

Her years were long and her eyes were failing, their brown gone grey with age. However, she did not need her eyes to see the things that others could not. She was one of the few Wise Elders of the villages that could rival Udrahdu Nabi in age. She has seen an untold number of monsoons, and was blessed with her mystic gifts for as long as anyone living could remember. After years of prayer, meditation, and discipline, Sunshadeen breathed into her and amplified her divine fire. Before going to battle, the chiefs would always ask her if there would be victory. She would never answer. She hated the violence. She would bless the war parties before they left, and pray for their safe return. What she prayed for most was a cessation to the conflict, though none seemed to be in sight. Many of the people in the twelve villages were tied to her line. Some were her grandchildren, others her great grandchildren. Others were the descendants of her nieces and nephews. Many of them were guided into the world by her gentle hands. Everyone that she called hers had slept by her fire and eaten from her pot. It grieved her to see that every time the war parties would leave, fewer of her kin would return. Likewise with every Jahisha attack, she was forced again to outlive more of her descendants. Life was precious to her, a lesson she did her best to impart in her teachings. Bhagir seemed to be the only one to listen.

"Can you save him, grandmother?" Bhagir asked, fiddling with the axe in his hand.

She continued to chant and wave smoke over the cat's body. She had crushed herbs and rubbed them into the wound and poured medicines into the feeble panther's mouth while Bhagir held it open. Bhagir had never been so close to a panther's jaws, and had he the choice, was not likely to repeat the experience.

Udrahdit Ru'a continued to chant and circle the hut, thickening the air with each wave of her hand. Suddenly she stopped. She placed the gourd on the ground, and sat cross legged in front of the panther. She placed her hand on the creature's head and closed her eyes.

"We are going to lose him Bhagir." She said.

Bhagir was confused. "But Tikursene told me to get him, to bring him here. Why would he have me do that when the panther was doomed to die?"

"Because there is only one thing that can save him." She turned and looked at her great grandson, shadows dancing on her face from hearth's flickering fire. "The gods are giving you this panther as a gift, but in order to prove that you are worthy, you must give one to him. You must give him some of your divine fire."

"My divine fire?" Bhagir furrowed his brow. "I don't understand."

"Will you do it?" Udrahdit Ru'a held out her hand.

Bhagir closed his eyes and sighed. "Yes."

"Then come, come quickly."

Bhagir did as he was told and took up a seat next to his great grandmother. Her hands were wreathed in white fire. She put one hand on the panther's head, and another on Bhagir's. Almost instantly Bhagir was nearly blinded by a flash of light, and before his eyes, in mere moments, he witnessed the entire life of the panther, from suckling cub to the terrifying beast he encountered after escaping the Jahisha. He felt the pain of every wound, the pleasure of every warm afternoon, and the cold of every wet monsoon. He tasted the blood of a fresh kill in his mouth, and the cold waters of the lake. Through the panther's eyes he chased a hare through the jungle and was startled by a man carrying weapons and covered in blood. He smelled of fear. They circled each other, then pain, then blackness.

"Bhagir." A familiar hand shook him by the shoulder. "Bhagir wake up the chiefs are gathering all the people together."

"How long was I asleep?" Bhagir rubbed the drowsiness from his eyes.

"Three days, my Wild Cat." Udrahdit Ru'a caressed his cheek. "You looked so peaceful, I did not want do disturb you."

"The panther?" He yawned.

"Gone, he belongs out there and not in here. The gods are pleased with you." She replied. "Come."

The night was uncommonly clear, almost as if the evening's glow had not given way to darkness. Bhagir stepped out of the hut holding on to his axe and Udrahdit Ru'a's arm in the other. He guided her to the fire at the centre of the village where the people gathered.

"Are we all here?" Asked Y'arit Ferris, the chief of this village. "Are we all gathered?"

This was the largest gathering Bhagir had seen in some time. The chiefs from every corner had come with all the warriors they could spare. They sat in a circle around the great fire in the village centre on wooden stools, the symbols of their authority. There was much mumbling and shuffling in the crowd.

Then, the cries for revenge began. Bhagir had learned listening to people that his village had been wiped out. None left behind had been left alive. Some of them may still be wandering the jungle in search of refuge, but their fate was unknown. The people wanted blood. One man stepped forward and cut his palm, dripping blood into the fire and demanding that they go immediately to avenge their kinsmen. The chiefs watched and listened for a moment, taking in the flood of emotions that washed over the clan.

"Everyone be still!" Y'arit Ferris stood tall with his arms out. His resemblance to Y'arit Ayoub, his elder brother, was uncanny. "Everyone be still. What has happened in our kinsman's village was worse than any other attack. It was pure unadulterated cowardice, and a great insult to the honour of our clan!"

"Every attack is an insult to the on honour of our clan!" Shouted one of the other chiefs. Bhagir did not recognize him. He was likely from one of the villages beyond the lake. "This must be answered with blood! What sort of coward sends snakes and scorpions to do his fighting for him?"

The people rumbled in agreement. They had been attacked before, this was nothing new. They were at war. What the chiefs would not admit was that the genius of the strategy used against them had hurt their pride. They needed to hit back and hit hard in order to regain honour and esteem among their kinsmen.

Bhagir scanned the crowd for signs of survivors from his village. He saw none. Perhaps the village was too tightly packed for him to recognize anyone in the sea of shadowed faces that surrounded him. He felt knots turning in his guts at the thought of what likely happened to his mother and siblings. His father was dead, he knew that much. His brothers would likely have been killed as well. He felt the rope around his wrists again. Visions of the scarred man's crime against his mother's honour repeated in his mind as vividly as if they were happening in front of his eyes. His heart slammed in his chest. There were no men left inside the village to defend her or his sisters. His mind turned to Selahst. Bhagir saw her father choke to death with a swollen face when the beehive broke. He remembered what his kinsmen had done to the Jahisha when they took their village. The thought of the same being visited upon those dearest to him made him sick to his stomach.

The chiefs prattled on; giving grand speeches about their individual exploits against the Jahisha: How many dozen they killed in combat, how many women they took as wives, the hides, precious stones, and smoked meat they claimed as the spoils of war, and whatever other embellishments they could proclaim to the night air. The Rahmineen shouted and ululated in praise of their bravery. Where the people saw courage, Bhagir saw barbarism. He knew now that he had no taste for blood. The gods had made his heart too soft. He let those women go, he would not leave the panther in the woods to die, and he almost died standing by his father in battle when told to run. Udrahdu Nabi was right; perhaps Bhagir would have made a better Wise Elder.

"Bhagir." A voice whispered his name.

"Grandmother did you say something?" He asked his elder. She shook her head and returned her attention to the speeches.

"Bhagir." The voice repeated again.

He looked around to see if someone was playing with him. Perhaps someone from his village had managed to escape the fighting and made their way to safety.

"Out." The voice said. "Out."

He slipped away from the crowd and made his way to the village gate. It was manned by several of his clansmen. They were large and had the faces of men that have cut down their fair share of foes. The small fire burning near them flickered, the light dancing against the contours of their well sculpted muscles.

"Where do you think you are going?" one of the men from down the river asked him.

"Out" the voice repeated in his head.

"I need to step out for a moment." Bhagir bowed his head as a sign of respect. He did not want to anger these giants.

"Why is that? What is waiting in the black of night for you?" Another one of them asked, his thick hands wringing the shaft of his ivory-tipped spear.

"I think that you will stay." Another replied, crossing his tree-trunk arms.

"Go back to the gathering and eat some of the meat. You will need it for the coming battle." Said another, his heavy war club resting on a thick shoulder.

Bhagir knew that they would not let him pass, and he did not want to be accused of spying for the Jahisha, so he backed away and looked for another way to leave the village. Beyond the bramble fence that surrounded the village and into the darkness, he saw the golden eyes waiting for him. Tikursene must have another message for him.

Bhagir wandered between the huts until he was out of sight, and walked along the fence. He was still unaccustomed to how bright the night had become. He searched the black sky to see the size of the moon, but he found only thinly veiled stars above him. Something was different, but he could not name it.

"Down" the voice said.

Bhagir scanned the bottom of the fence and found a small gap between the stacks of thorny bush. He lay on his belly, flattened himself and axe in hand, crawled through. It was moments like these that he was grateful for his slender frame. When he rose to his feet, he saw Tikursene standing before him, clear as the dimming afternoon. Before he could utter a word, the guardian turned and ran into the undergrowth.

"Follow." The voice of the guardian spoke.

Bhagir obeyed, he ran after the giant jungle cat. His heart raced along with his feet as he sprinted behind his guide. A rush that raised the hair on the back of his neck overcame him. It permeated his every fibre as he ran behind Tikursene through the jungle. The closer he came to catching up, the faster Tikursene ran. The faster Tikursene ran, the faster Bhagir would run. He felt like he was flying, his feet were light and quiet as he whipped through the undergrowth with a speed he never knew he had. Suddenly the running stopped.

Bhagir stood beside Tikursene, kneeling down to match his crouching posture. He followed the guardian's gaze and cast his eyes upon a small encampment. The fires were dying and the men were preparing to sleep. Their captives, however, were far from rested. It took a moment for Bhagir to realize what he was looking at, a perceptive ambiguity that was rapidly cleared by the sound of his mother's weeping. Blood fire welled up inside of him. Those captives were the people of his village, those men were the bastards that tricked his kinsmen into slaughter. This could not stand, but there were too many.

"Why did you bring me here to see this?" Bhagir whispered.

There was no answer. Bhagir turned his face to Tikursene and found nothing but leaves swaying in the breeze.

"Hunt." A voice said.

Bhagir knew what he had to do. He surveyed the camp and counted the men. There were too many. He could never take them all himself. Stealth would have to be his weapon. Low on his belly he crawled through the bushes around them, watching. Bhagir saw two men guarding the prisoners. They were too large. He could not fight them both alone, and the noise would raise the entire camp against him. He watched and waited as one fire died and the other ebbed to barely a flicker. Common sense told Bhagir that he should leave. He could run back and call the warriors to find the Jahisha war party here, but he could not bring himself to leave. They may be gone by the time the Rahmineen arrived. His mother was in sight; next to her was his sister Neferudya. His youngest sister Shaiadahna and his brothers were not among the captives. He feared the worst, but could not allow for grief to overtake him. What family he had left needed his help.

He took to his feet and then crouched low, his footfalls were silent, and the great hanging leaves barely moved as he brushed past them. He had to get behind the guards. Round the edge of the camp he crept, eyes fixed on the guards and their captives. Eventually he found himself behind them, close enough to pounce. Still, neither the guards, nor their barely sleeping captives were aware of his presence. He watched them and he waited. He had to kill them quietly, but even if he was fast enough to take them, any noise they would make would be the end of him. On the other edge of the encampment there was movement in the bushes, vigorous and unconcerned with discretion.

"Something in the bushes there." One of them pointed with his chin.

"Better be careful when you go out to the bushes to stroke your cock." The other snickered.

"Fuck you then, I don't need to stroke my cock. Y'arit Zalaru gave me the prettiest one in the village for throwing that beehive."

"Which one was that?" the first man wrinkled his nose.

"See that one over there?" The second man pointed to a girl tied apart from the rest. "I killed three men to get at her. There was one with a big head that put up a real fight. I gutted him like a deer." He pulled the knife from his waist band and mocked a stabbing motion. "I haven't tasted her yet, I'll wait until I get her home and I can make her one of my wives."

"That's four captures isn't it?" Said the first.

His comrade nodded proudly. Bhagir's stomach turned. Now he knew where his friends had gone and he suspected that he knew the identity of that girl tied off apart from the others.

The bushes on the other side of the camp rustled again. The guards stood up, weapons at the ready. Whatever it was, it was large.

From the undergrowth emerged a familiar creature, the panther that Bhagir and his great grandmother saved from the snake bite. The guards were at a loss as to how to react. The panther did not charge them, nor did he keep his distance. He just looked at them, daring them with his eyes as they glimmered in the light of the fire. The panther crept toward the tiny flame, sniffed at it, and then smothered it with dirt, blanketing the camp in darkness.

"Why did he do that?" Said the first guard. "I can't see a thing!"

"I am going to kill that stupid cat." Said the other. "Throw some kindling on it before the embers die."

Bhagir could not understand why they were complaining. The fire was gone, but the light was not. He could see them plainly before him.

"Hunt." A voice whispered. The panther looked at him and darted off into the night.

Not another word was needed. Bhagir took a deep breath, and threw himself forward. His axe struck down the first of the guards. The man's skull cracked open and his body hit the ground with a thud.

"Ahmose. What was that?" The other guard said with his arms outstretched, searching blindly for his comrade. "Ahmose?"

The panther did not give Bhagir the opportunity to finish the second guard. In the blink of an eye the cat was on him, fangs buried deep into his bleeding throat. In a few quiet gasps, he was gone. Bhagir watched his new companion pull a mouth full of flesh from the guard's neck and drop it beside his trembling carcass. There was no reaction from Bhagir's kin. It was as if they could not see what had happened, and then he understood. Sharing his divine fire with the panther gave him the sight, speed, and silence of the animal. Sunshadeen granted him these gifts as a reward for the kindness he showed the creature.

"What is happening?" his mother's voice trembled in the darkness. "Who is out there?"

"Be silent mother. I am here." Bhagir whispered.

He took the knife from the waistband of one of the fallen men and cut his mother's restraints. Her trembling hands searched for his embrace. Bhagir took hold of her hands and pulled her to him. Her tears wet his shoulder.

"Your brothers, your sister…" She choked through her poorly stifled sobs.

"Hush." Bhagir kissed her on the forehead and pressed the flint knife in her hand. "Help me cut the others free."

As quickly as their hands and feet would allow them, Bhagir and his mother freed the other captives from their bonds.

"Selahst" Bhagir whispered as he cut her bonds. "It's me, Bhagir."

"Bhagir? Where are you?"

He placed a hand on her shoulder. She flinched as if he was about to strike her. Bhagir dragged the bark cord against the edge of his weapon. Her restraints gone, she quietly embraced him with tearful gratitude.

A sudden bright flash of light shattered the darkness that concealed them. Bhagir shielded his eyes as he turned around. The camp fires burned brightly, rekindled by some unseen force. The Jahisha war party was awake. A menacing warrior holding a long spear in one hand and a war club in the other stood before the flames, his kinsmen on either side of him with weapons in hand.

"Bhagir, your eyes." Selahst's mouth gaped in astonishment. "What? How?"

Bhagir's eyes flashed like polished stones against the firelight.

"Rise, O sons of Jahi, your prizes are escaping." The Jahisha chieftain growled. "Bring to me the head of that one with the glowing eyes. I want to mount it on a stake in front of my hut."

Bhagir took up his weapon and faced his foes. Now was not the time to run, now was not the time to stand awestruck at the deadly ballet of combat. Now was the time to stand and fight.

"If you seek to capture them again, then you must come through me. I warn you, if you do come, Sunshadeen may soon follow to claim your divine fire!"

"Bhagir, run!" Kahina begged him. "Run, my son!"

Selahst rose to her feet and tugged at his bloody weapon hand. "Please come with us."

"No, you run." Bhagir's blood was on fire. "They cannot follow if they are dead."

With that, he raised his axe high and charged forward, bellowing thunder from his chest, the panther close behind. His foes charged forth in kind. Bhagir leapt over the corpse of his first victim, and returning to the earth split the skull of the first man to approach him. The smell of the blood excited him as never before. He felt the wildness of the panther in him. While he tried to pull the axe out of the skull of the man he felled, another came behind him with a spear. The panther saw to it that the spear never reached his new companion. Bhagir's next opponent thrusted a stone spear point at his face. One of Bhagir's hands bat the shaft aside and the other replied with a savage swing of the liberated axe to the throat. The Jahisha warrior tried to cover the gaping wound, but collapsed before his hands could reach it.

Such was the manner in which the melee unfolded. As fast as they came for him, Bhagir was faster still. He was faster, stronger, unstoppable. The panther fought beside him ferociously, making full use of every weapon endowed him by nature. Bhagir roared his bloodlust into the night as he and the panther cut them down, casting their bodies at Bhagir's blood-soaked feet like over ripe fruit fallen from broken stems. Bhagir and panther the stood there, panting over their twisted corpses, baptized in their blood. He turned his burning gaze to the menacing figure with the spear and the war club. He was the last man standing, yet he looked unafraid.

"I do not know how a creature like you crawled out of the Sunbaka, but I will send you back." He snarled. With a shout to the heavens, his Ra wreathed his weapons and hands in white flame.

The panther snarled and ran into the jungle at the sight of the chieftain's Ra. Bhagir was alone. He locked eyes with his adversary, who now advanced toward him with sure, steady steps, the rage in his gaze as hot as the white flames he held. Bhagir squeezed axe, and reached around his feet, finding another axe.

With a shout of rage, Bhagir unleased a flurry of strikes at his opponent. He swung for the Jahisha's head, thigh, ribs, neck, shoulder and groin. Each attack was fruitless; all of his blows met with a parry that nearly shook the haft from Bhagir's grip. Each time their weapons connected, there was a bright flash of white light that stung Bhagir's eyes. His opponent took his turn, thrusting with the spear point and hammering at him with the war club. Bhagir used his newfound speed as best he could and avoided the blows as they came. The Jahisha chieftain's weapons gave chase.

While the Jahisha warrior was distracted with the task of killing Bhagir, the panther snuck through the bushes around the camp and from behind Bhagir's opponent, charged for the kill. Before the panther could leap at him, the Jahisha whipped around and threw a ball of the white flame from his hand at the panther, sending him running back to the brush.

"Stop jumping around!" The Jahisha shouted in rage as his spear point chased after Bhagir. One of his missed blows ran through the corpse of his kinsman, hissing as it plunged into his back.

Bhagir kept moving, muttering prayers to the gods that his new gifts would be enough to preserve him. Few are the men that survived a bellicose encounter with a warrior bearing the white flame. Bhagir saw an opportunity and flew forward, seeking to end this fight with a blow to the head. His axe head was caught by a parry with the war club, and the Jahisha thrusted his spear for Bhagir's belly. The young warrior's immediate reaction was to let go of his bound weapon and take the spear by the shaft. His hand hissed and burned as he reached into the flame and took hold of the spear just behind its point. He gritted his teeth and growled in pain as he pushed the point away from his tender belly.

The Jahisha thrusted with his spear again. Bhagir deflected the blow with his axe and fell backwards. His agility failed him. Before he had a chance to recover, an angry war club came down on his shoulder. The Jahisha was aiming for his head, but he was more angry than accurate. The pain was unbelievable. The skin of Bhagir's shoulder sizzled and bubbled in the place where the Jahisha struck him. Again came the spear point. Bhagir grabbed the burning shaft with both hands this time as the Jahisha pressed it forward, trying to drive the point into Bhagir's heart. The flesh of his hands hissed as he held the shaft for dear life. Bhagir watched the skin burn away from his hands as his grip faltered and the spear point inched ever closer to his pounding chest.

"All glory to the gods!" Bhagir exclaimed, appealing to them for strength. "All glory to Sun, all glory to Sunshaia, all glory to Sunshadeen!"

"Invoke the gods till your heart's content. Then I will pierce it." The Jahisha dropped his war club and put all of his weight behind the spear.

The point of the spear was now burning at the skin in the centre of Bhagir's chest. Bhagir roared and pressed the spear back again. His grip weakening on the shaft, he felt it slipping through his hands. He continued to repeat exaltations to the gods as he held fast. He was not ready for his divine fire to return to Sun's halo. He refused to die like this. The spear came closer, this time the point began to sear past the first layer of his skin. This was it, his strength was sapped, and the Jahisha was bent on ending his life. His mind emptied, and he prepared himself to let go and let Sunshadeen claim his divine fire.

"All glory to Sunshadeen." He whispered, ready to accept his fate, but this was not to be.

As soon as the last syllable of the mantra passed between his lips Bhagir felt a surge of energy overtake his body. The white flame of the Jahisha's spear no longer burned his hands. The strength in his grip returned and every fibre of his being was filled with an ecstasy he had never known possible. He looked up at the Jahisha that stood over him, his eyes now white as the flame, his whole body swathed in sacred fire. Bhagir pushed the spear back and rose to his feet, still holding the shaft as the head pointed to his chest. The enemy grimaced and pressed harder, but to no avail. Ra was strong in Bhagir's bloodline, and his had just awoken. Bhagir pushed the spear aside and took hold of his foe in attempt to throw him to the ground. A more experienced fighter, the Jahisha shook himself free and reclaimed his spear. Bhagir took his axes up and again they circled each other.

Each man advanced and withdrew, testing the defences of the other. Every time their weapons clashed, the power of their Ra flashed brighter than a thousand fires. The Jahisha grew impatient and committed to a full thrust at Bhagir's belly. In one smooth motion, Bhagir hooked the spear shaft under the head of one axe while he came down into his foe's shoulder with the other, splitting open and burning the flesh. He followed with a second blow to the neck, and finally to the side of his shaven head, cracking it open like an ostrich egg and quenching his divine fire.

Bhagir looked over the corpse of his fallen foe, light now extinguished. He examined his own body wreathed in his divine fire. The gods had blessed him, giving him not only the powers of a panther, but they also amplified his divine fire. Few were granted this gift, and now he was among them. He looked at his axes, stained with the blood of his fallen foes. The jungle was quiet now. The sounds of battle had faded like an animal skulking into the shadows to die. The axes fell from his hands, then Bhagir fell to his knees, and he wept. He thanked the gods for their gifts; he thanked them for the strength to save his mother, his sister, Selahst, and the other captives. He prayed for his fallen kin, and still he wept into his upturned palms, washing the blood of his enemies away in his catharsis.

"Bhagir." A voice called to him.

He sniffled and looked in the direction of the sound. The panther had emerged from the jungle again, Tikursene standing behind him. The guardian motioned to the panther.

"Dahnasene, your divine fire." He then left the two of them alone in the camp, accompanied only by the choir of singing crickets.

"Dahnasene." Bhagir nodded.

"Come." Dahnasene's voice whispered in his head.

He was right, his mother, his sister, and the rest of his kin were still in the jungle. Bhagir rose to his feet, took up the axes, and both he and Dahnasene darted off into the jungle to find the lost and bring them home.

<u>**Epilogue**</u>

"Where have you two been?" Nabila stood at the village gate, a scowl on her face and her arms akimbo. "You told me you would return before Sun painted the sky! I was ready to send a war party out to look for you."

"And as you can see, Sun is still in the sky, and the horizon remains unpainted." Khufu grinned at his daughter in law, A'azgimai asleep in his arms. "However, a certain precious star of ours seems to have decided that her day is done."

Nabila stretched out her hands and took the sleeping child, who facilitated the exchange by reaching drowsily for her mother and returning to sleep on her shoulder. "Her hands are sticky."

"Eating half a bee's nest of honeycomb and then half an ostrich egg's worth on the way home will do that to a child." The old man chuckled.

Nabila shook her head and led her father in law back into the village. "The Y'arit was looking for you."

"He is always looking for me. What does my son want?"

"Udrahdu Ullah came from the other side of the lake. He looked rather shaken." She whispered as they passed between the huts, the air about them thick with the smoke of cooking fires.

"Was his village attacked by raiders?" Udrahdu Khufu's voice lowered so as not to raise any alarm.

"No, but he says something worse has happened." She replied. "That is what I heard at least. He has sent for the other chiefs and the Wise Elders from the neighbouring villages and even those down the river to the coast."

"Is it war again with the Jahisha?"

Nabila pointed to the great hut near the village centre. "Rasul can tell you more. He waits for you there."

Khufu kissed Nabila and A'azgimai each on the forehead and made his way to the great hut. There he found his son, Y'arit Rasul sitting next to a still visibly shaken Udrahdu Ullah, who rocked back and forth, counting the clay beads on the string with his fingers.

"Peace and blessings be upon both of you." Khufu put a hand over his chest and bowed in greeting.

"Peace and blessings father." Rasul kissed his father's hand respectfully.

Udrahdu Ullah kept rocking. Khufu leaned his staff against the wall and set a stool between his son and their guest.

"Ullah." He whispered. "What troubles you, O kin of mine? What leaves you shaken so?"

Ullah did not answer; he only looked at his fellow Udrahdu with pleading eyes and kept rocking.

Khufu looked at his son. "Has he been like this since he arrived?"

"Yes, father. He barely spoke when he arrived at our gate; he simply repeated the darkness has crossed over. I have my suspicions as to what he meant, but I am no Wise Elder, Ra or no."

"Ullah. Ullah! Harken to me!"

Udrahdu Ullah's head jerked to Udrahdu Khufu's direction.

Khufu closed his eyes and breathed deeply "All glory to the gods." White flame wreathed his body. Khufu placed his hands on Ullah's shaven head. "Look into my eyes and let me in."

Ullah's eyes opened wide as he moaned in terror.

"Tell me what you saw."

Through his mind's eye, Khufu saw visions of what terrified his fellow Wise Elder. It all happened so fast. Bodies swathed in black mist threw down the brave warriors that faced them. The bravest men were wrought to feral madness when that black mist dove down their throats. The carnage that ensued was more savage than the wrath of any war party. One of those bodies wreathed in that black mist turned to Ullah and lunged at him. Khufu severed the connection. His back was soaked in cold sweat.

"What did you see, father?" Y'arit Rasul asked.

"The darkness that turned brother against brother and caused the Great Divide has found a servant." Khufu's voice trembled. "We are not ready.

THE GREAT DIVIDE

<u>Prologue</u>

The night air was alive in the streets of Bakar. The atmosphere was heavy with the scent of roasting meat, singing poets, and playing musicians. It had been ten years since the end of the War of the Dzinee, ten years since the atmosphere was thick with the fetor of rot and desperation. It had been ten years since city walls were painted in the blood of the fallen while the bloodthirsty Mazkhee[11] roamed the smouldering ruins, feasting on the flesh of the dead and dying. Celebrations were in order. King Dedu had not only restored order to the land and safeguarded the Bakari, but he led the reconstruction of their great city. He rewarded himself with a great pyramid in the city centre. The city state's farms produced great bounty, and none dared come against their walls. Their towers and ziggurats were almost as beautiful as those in the city of Dzakira. The Dark Sages guarded the city jealously, and their Dzinee thralls greedily devoured anyone who would dare question the power of the king or the spiritual authority of the sages that upheld his crown.

"Move aside! Make way!" shouted the captain, waving his baton at the throngs of festival goers.

As the people saw who came behind him, they immediately crushed to the side of the road and knelt. A procession of red-cloaked warriors preceded the great sage Tikurkebre. He sat in a golden sedan chair held high by the scaly shoulders of his chained Barukdzin[12] thralls.

"Make way for the Great Sage!" The captain shouted again as the crowd continued to part.

Tikurkebre waved his bejewelled cow tail switch and called the dark favour of the Sunbaka on those who bowed before him. His brow sloped low under his red conical turban, nearly the same colour as the henna that dyed the forked beard jutting forth from his jaw. His slender frame hid under the mass of fine black linen robes

---

[11] Also known as "turned ones", people who drink the blood of the Dzinee and become misshapen creatures that thirst for human blood

[12] A class of Dzinee, creatures created from the corruption of nature in the name of war

that swathed him in authoritative opulence. He was a lover of the arts, and never failed to be among the people when celebrations were afoot. He had a seat awaiting him at his favourite playhouse, and the show would not begin until he arrived. His procession of guards, monsters, and acolytes continued through the spreading crowd.

"Ibebi! No!" A voice called out.

Tikurkebre turned his head to the noise, and a he saw a father running behind his child, who with reckless abandon chased his ball from among the people and into the formation of armed guards.

"Close formation!" The captain shouted.

Without hesitation, the guards turned outwards and packed themselves in shoulder to shoulder, spears forward. The father of the wayward child stopped abruptly when a spear point blocked his path and nearly pierced his eye. Immediately, he threw himself down and begged forgiveness.

"Please I am sorry." His voice trembled, forehead on the ground. "Please let me take my son and I will go. I beg your forgiveness, O Great Sage!"

The captain stormed over to him, the scales in his armour chinking with each step. Without breaking stride he heaved a sandaled foot into the ribs of the trembling man, winding him and leaving him curled up on his side and gasping for air.

"Control your brat!" He sneered as he struck him with a baton. "Do you know the penalty for running at the Great Sage?"

"Abbu[13]!" The Ibebi ran over, his ball in hand. The boy positioned himself between his father and the captain's baton. "LEAVE MY ABBU!" The child gave the captain a push.

The captain cocked his arm back. "You little..."

"Stop." The Great Sage raised an open hand.

The captain stayed his hand.

"If you kill them, O Captain, then there will be two less people to praise the Sunbaka." His voice was deep and his speech was measured. "Bring them hither."

---

[13] Father

The captain waved to his guards, who scooped up the gasping man and dragged him to the Great Sage.

"*Fut*[14]" Tikurkebre commanded his Barukdzin.

They lowered the sedan char to the ground and the Great Sage rose to his feet. He was uncommonly tall, and looked down upon the man, who knelt before him, his son in his arms.

"What is your name?" Tikurkebre's voice grumbled.

"S-s-Shadin, O Great Sage. This is my son Ibebi."

"Do you know the power of the Sunbaka?" The Great Sage presented his ring, a bloodstone in the gaping mouth of a cobra.

Shadin kissed the ring, and directed his son to do the same. "Yes, O Great Sage. Its power keeps us safe."

"Do you surrender to it?"

"With all my heart." He was lying.

Without a word, the Great Sage returned to his seat. "*Fit*[15]" He commanded in the Old Tongue.

The Barukdzin lifted the sedan chair.

"Captain, take them to the ziggurat. Have them taste of the sacred blood. Bless them with the gift of the Sunbaka's power." Tikurkebre waved the cow tail switch in their general direction.

"No."

"What was that?" The captain growled. "You are about to be blessed with the sacred blood, how can you refuse?"

"NO!" Shadin stood up, his son in his arms. "You will not give that to my son! You will not turn us into Mazkeen!"

The peasant shook himself free of the grip of the Great Sage's guards and backed towards the crowd.

"This is a farce, this is all a farce! You are no sacred leader, you are a butcher!" He shouted. "A butcher!"

Shadin's shouts of condemnation were silenced by a hard fist to his mouth, knocking out several of his teeth and robbing him of his footing. Ibebi fell from his father's arms, and his father fell into the

---

14 Down
15 Up

arms of a pair of guards, who quickly bound his hands and kicked him into submission.

"Abbu!" Ibebi shouted with an outstretched arm.

"WAIT!" A brave voice shouted from the crowd. "WAIT!"

The captain stomped forward and took the protestor by the throat. "You better have a damned good reason to interrupt the Great Sage's justice. I have half a mind..."

"You sure do! Now, you could do all kinds of nasty things to poor old me, but then you would rob the Great Sage of his evening's entertainment." He smiled. "I am Ghazi, have been sent by the master of the playhouse to ensure our tall, dark, and ominous patron's comfortable enjoyment of tonight's play."

"You are full of shit." The captain tightened his grip. "I think I'll just choke you right here."

Ghazi tried to gargle something between gasps as he pointed down the street.

"Release him Captain Shahad." The Great Sage ordered.

Captain Shahad bowed his head and released their guide.

"I was trying to say, O Captain Squeeze Hands, that the Dagudzin's Head is just over there and we have prepared our finest table for the Great Sage in the gallery. If you will follow me please?" Ghazi rubbed his throat and forced a smile.

"Leave him, let us go to the show." Tikurkebre waved at his men.

The guards left little Ibebi to weep over his battered father. The procession followed Ghazi's lead to the polished oak doors of the Dagudzin's Head, the finest playhouse in Bakar. Preceded by his guards and followed by his acolytes and Barukdzin, Tikurkebre walked into the darkened playhouse and up the stairs to his seat in the gallery. A feast was laid out before him. Steaming cuts of hyena meat, fresh fruit, and baked fare hot from the cook's oven covered the great table. Ghazi bowed low. "Is this to your liking, O Great Sage?"

Tikurkebre took his seat, crossed his legs and nodded his head. "Begin the show."

"You heard His Darkness! Begin the show!" Ghazi shouted down from the gallery.

A poet stepped out to centre stage, clad in a black robe, her face hidden under a hood. The room was silent. She raised her slender brown arms above her head and began.

"Ladies and gentlemen, esteemed guests! Here we are gathered to share with you the stories of our ancient past. Of days before brick and mortar, fire and metal, before we knew glory and sacrifice! Yea, lend me your ears, O people, and tonight we shall weave for you great tales of broken hearts and unfulfilled promises. Harken to us, O people, for we have a story to tell."

Imsaid's Desire

(~14,000 years before the War of Banishment)

I loved her. Her smile was the beauty of all creation. She was light, she was life, and she was my beloved. Nothing in my life could rival her beauty. Her midnight hair curled like the waves of the sea, her skin was flawless onyx, and her eyes were deep pools of splendour that begged me to drown each time I beheld them. O Yahuia! She was my one desire, and for her love I would have died a thousand deaths.

I lived by the sea with all of Sun's people. Sunshaia's gift never ceased to provide for us all that we needed. Never did we hunger, for there was always fish near the shore, and there was always seaweed dancing on sandy seabed begging to be harvested. We lived by the grace of the gods, and in their worship we found harmony. The patriarchs of our village kept us faithful and reminded us of the gratitude we owed to those that created for us. When Sun sat on high in the sapphire sky and the warmth caressed our backs, we gave thanks. When the rains came down and filled the rivers with fresh water for us to drink, we gave thanks. When we lit the fires that warmed us at night and cooked our food we gave thanks.

My brother and I spent our days on the beach, paddling our reed boats over the crystal waters with our harpoons, searching for the next day's meal. When our smoke house was full of fish, we swam. When we tired of swimming, we ran along the beach, our feet slapping against the wet sand as we chased each other under the light of our gods.

Izkah was my other half. We were twins, and Elder Rahi said that twins always share a divine fire. It was hard to disagree when we shared a face. He was quieter than me. He was always deep in thought and asking questions, sometimes the questions he would ask would bring him more trouble than the knowledge was worth. Once he asked Elder Jahi a question about opposites.

"If there is both light and dark, hot and cold, fullness and hunger, wet and dry, O Elder, what then is the opposite of Sun?" he once asked.

Elder Jahi's answer was a cane to the thigh. "Never ask questions like that again. The gods gave us everything we need, and we should never think to ask for the opposite. The opposite of life is death, why would you seek it out?"

The answer was not satisfactory, but the soreness in Izkah's thigh signalled that he would not find a different answer if he were to ask again.

"Izakah, why are you limping?" I asked him.

"I will give you three guesses." He replied.

I poked at the tender flesh of his thigh. "I think I will only need one. Elder Jahi is a liberal one with that cane."

Izkah swatted my hand away. "Stop pressing at it. For someone who shares a divine fire with me, you are terrible at sharing my pain."

"Izkah, you are my pain." I laughed. "I suppose there is no running or swimming for you today."

"That is fine by me. You run your mouth enough for the both of us."

"Your jokes are terrible." I offered him my arm.

"And so is your breath." He chuckled.

I furrowed my brow, then opened my mouth wide and breathed hotly into his grimacing face. "Come on, we are all making rope cutting wood in the centre of the village. The village is gathered to build a hut for Yunus and Yara's unborn baby. Yahuia is going to be there."

"Yes she is." Izkah smiled at the mention of her name. For all that I knew of my brother, I should have known that there was something in his heart for her. How could there not have been? She was perfect.

The village centre was a beehive of activity. Some of the men had already brought stones to help with the foundation, while the elder men got together to split saplings and strip bark for the rope the women braided. They all sang as they worked. Sun's people always sang. We sang when we were happy, we sang when the Sunshadeen came to claim the old, we sang when we married, and we sang when new babies were born. We sang when we worked, we sang when we played, we even sang ourselves to sleep. What good is a voice if not to sing?

"Izkah! Imsaid!" There was that voice, sweeter than any birdsong the gods could compose.

"Yahuia!" We said in unison.

She came to us with her arms outstretched and embraced us both. Her hair smelled of flowers.

"You heard the news! I am going to be an elder sister!" She grinned. "I hope this time it is a girl. My parents produce nothing but boys." She looked at us and winked. "Not that there is anything wrong with that. Come! My father needs help collecting clay for the walls and palm leaves for the roof."

"Another baby." I said. "Do your parents know when to quit?"

Izkah looked at me, scolding my rudeness with his eyes. "Imsaid…"

"Izkah, what happened to your leg?" Yahuia changed the subject and poked at his thigh.

"Elder Jahi" we said in unison again.

"You asked him something silly again didn't you?" Yahuia shook her head. "Izkah when will you ever learn?"

"That is exactly what I want to do Yahuia, I want to learn.

There are so many things that we do not know. Why does Sun cross the sky? Why does Sunshaia weep to send us water from that same sky? Why can we drink from the river and not the sea? I want to know things; I want to know the world for more than what we see on the surface." He answered proudly. "And every lump that I earn in that quest is worth the exchange."

"Try to avoid getting too many more lumps. The Choosing Ceremony is coming soon and I would not want for you to damage that handsome face and ruin your prospects for a wife." She poked his cheek before abandoning us to return to her work.

"She said I was handsome." I smiled.

"She was talking to me Imsaid."

"Well you are an uglier version of me, so if she calls you handsome, then it means I am even more handsome than that."

"Sometimes I wonder about you. How is your head so empty?"

My head wasn't empty, it was full of her.

"Izkah, your leg is too tender to haul stones or tread clay. Go and make fibre for rope and I will help our father and the others with the clay and stone."

"I can still help." Izkah stood erect, his hands on his hips.

I smirked at him. "Catch me then." I tapped his tender thigh and ran.

Izkah winced and his knee bent. "Fine! I will make rope!" He shouted to me as I ran laughing to the clay pit.

I loved my brother.

I arrived at the clay pit as the men hauled earth up by the armfull and wrapped them in skins to carry to the village on their heads.

"Imsaid!" It was Dawish, my broad-chested cousin and Elder Jahi's favourite grandson. "Showing up just when the work is ending as always!"

I jumped into the pit with both feet. They had dug down to where the clay was moist, and coaxed by some seawater, it was easy to form and pry from the bosom of the earth. My landing left deep impressions of my feet in the pit. "Well the work is not done, and so no man can say that I never put a hand in."

Dawish took a muddy hand and wiped it on my arm. "Now you look like you've done some work. Now come, help us get these last few loads up. We need to get this hut built for Yunus and Yara so that we can prepare for the Choosing Ceremony."

"You act like anyone is interested in making you their choice." I chuckled.

Dawish laughed and flexed his arms. "Look at my muscle, you can't find a beast roaming our green grasses this strong."

"Or that stupid." Sometimes I say things before I tell myself not to say them.

I tried to climb out of the pit, but Dawish caught my foot. The two of us laughed as he pulled me back down and shellacked more clay on my back.

"You two! Are you helping or are you going to roll around in the mud like kibokeen[16]?"

"Sorry, father." I replied.

"My apologies Uncle." Dawish bowed his head.

My father was a serious man. His braids were never out of place, and his facial hair was always well shaped. "Come on up and help us haul the last of this clay. Then Imsaid, I have some more work for you." He reached out a hand to pull me up.

"Yes, father." I took his hand climbed from the pit.

We saw to bringing the rest of the clay back and created a great pile of it near the building site. Many of the poles and crossbeams had already been set and lashed, though there was still much work to be done. Sun was painting the sky and it was getting too late to place the stones and build up the walls. That would have to wait until tomorrow. While the fish was set to cook on the fire, my father thought that it was a good idea to put me to more work, since he felt the singular bundle of clay I carried was not helping enough. He sent me to haul stones to set in the walls until it was time to eat. I had to produce ten of the largest stones that I could carry, and then I would be free. Everyone else was able to wash themselves in the sea and rest before dinner, but not I. By the time my father was satisfied with my punishment, I was covered from sole to crown in dirt. I was glad for the mercy when he finally gave me leave to wash.

I stood waist deep in the cleansing tide of the endless water as Sun crossed over the horizon. My body ached, and I somewhat regretted not making rope with Izkah and Yahuia. I sank into the waves, my mind swimming with thoughts of her. I dreamed of her hands caressing my body, her lips touching mine, her breasts pressed against me. I lost myself in thoughts of her, and in my solitude I

---

[16] Hippopotami

indulged the fantasy beneath the water. I let the water lap against me, imagining that it was her, whispering sweet nothings. I breathed deeply, if only.

"Imsaid."

My head shot up and I looked around for the voice that called my name. I hid myself beneath the waves and searched.

"Imsaid, supper will be ready soon, and Elder Rahmi is singing the Song of Creation."

It was Yahuia. I closed my eyes and silently screamed for Sunshadeen to take me there and then. The embarrassment was more than I could bear.

"By and by I will come. I would not want to miss that. Elder Rahmi has the truest voice I have ever heard." I lied, hers was the truest voice.

"Then come!" She beckoned me. "Unless you want to spend the whole night in the water."

"Go ahead, I will follow you." I waved to her.

Not one to be shooed away, Yahuia walked into the water and took my arm.

"Come." Something was different in the way that she looked at me.

I closed my eyes and prayed for the calming of my nature as I stood up. Sunshaia was kind and hid my shame. Yahuia looked upon my nakedness and paused.

"Imsaid, I need to tell you something."

"What is it?"

"I know who I am going to choose at the ceremony."

My heart sank. "You aren't supposed to tell. The women never say who they will choose until it is time."

"I think that it is important that you know." She looked up at me, her eyes shining into mine through the darkness. "I choose you."

Words were stolen from my lips. I could not answer.

"Are you not going to say anything Imsaid?" She sounded hurt. "Are you even going to ask me why?"

"I-I, there are smarter men, there are stronger men." I replied. "Dawish is a mountain, my brother is..."

She put a finger over my mouth and silenced me. "I want you because you don't think you are good enough. You will love me. I will be more than just a wife to you. I will be your life."

She kissed me. I never thought that fire could live under water. She showed me that it could. The act of free love was no crime among us. Love existed for its own sake. Our bodies engaged in the ancient dance of life. Her hands caressed my body; her lips touched mine, her breasts pressed against me. The waves lapped against us as we swayed to the rhythm of our desire. I lost myself in the moment, and we lost ourselves in each other. The apex of her ecstasy was a song from her divine fire, a melody composed by the gods. We sang together.

She told me that she loved me.

We returned to the circle as Elder Rahmi finished the song. We sat on opposite sides of the fire and ate our meal, holding the secret of our union like an unborn child in the womb of our patience. The days were counting down. At the ceremony she would make her choice known and our love official. We only needed to be patient. Until then, we would steal away together in the night and commune as lovers do.

When the hut was finally complete, the three patriarchs gathered and blessed the fruit of our cooperation. We always did this together. We welcomed new life together, and bid farewell to those that passed together. We were our strength. We were the world. The gods created us to be together, and together we were beautiful children of the earth. We sang and clapped our hands, our voices exalting the divine and declaring our love for one another. As we sang, Yahuia and I could not keep from watching each other. Tomorrow would be the ceremony, and she would choose me. Tomorrow could not come fast enough.

Izkah, however, seemed to be uninterested in the Choosing Ceremony, as he was with most things that involved other people. He sat by himself and did not partake in the singing.

"Izkah!" I shouted. "Come and sing with us!"

My brother simply waved me off and walked away. Only the gods knew what was in his heart, he seemed troubled, but could not be bothered to say. While the rest of the people clapped and sang,

Yahuia and I stole away to make love again. Before long, we would be married, and we would no longer have to hide.

"Tomorrow." She whispered as she kissed me.

"Tomorrow."

I barely slept that night. I stared at the roof of the childhood hut I shared with my brother, the one we were born and raised in together. Soon I would be looking at the roof of my own hut, with her sleeping next to me instead of my snoring brother. I coaxed myself to sleep, whispering her name as slumber took me away.

The sound of a ram's horn blasted me from my slumber as Sun rose to paint the sky. Elder Rahmi was rousing the village to prepare for the ceremony. The day had come. The unmarried girls painted their skin with swirling white patterns that mimicked the waves of the endless waters in honour of Sunshaia. Around their waists they donned their finest grass skirts. They tied rattles to their ankles and spread their thick hair as wide as they could. We bachelors painted our bodies with red ochre, patterned in images of fire on our skin in honour of Sunshadeen. We tied rattles to our feet and wore cloaks of woven bark fibre and grass.

We met in the village centre just as Sun had reached the summit of the clear azure above us. The dancing began. The singing in the ceremony always started with the Song of Creation, when Sunshaia, the water goddess, and Sunshadeen the fire god, conspired to create all life. This was an ancient dance, a rite that persisted long before any of us or our grandmothers could remember. Before the women could make their choices, we all had to dance in exaltation of the gods and in remembrance of our ancestors.

A great dancer I was not, but I put on the best show that I could, pretending to dance for all of the unmarried women. I stomped my feet in front of Layla, and flipped my cloak in front of A'azgimai. I felt like everyone knew that I was pretending. Izkah took his turn and danced before the women; he bowed before Yahuia, and paid passing notice to the others. A'azgimai watched him dance before Yahuia and did her best to hide her characteristic scowl of disappointment. Perhaps I should have said something to my brother. Dawish stepped forward with his trademark bravado, beating his chest and flexing his muscles as he kicked dust into the air. Though his physique was impressive, his dancing was too out of pace with the music, and seemed to incite more laughter than excitement. The other young men took their turns before we conceded the field to the ladies.

The young women did not disappoint. Between the oscillations of their hips and sureness of their steps, it was no wonder that the goddess manifested in the steady flow of water. The elder women ululated as their younger counterparts repeated the same steps they made so many years ago. The unmarried women each danced in turn, but I cared for only one of them. My eyes craved Yahuia. I marvelled at the effortless grace of her dance, her grass skirt swaying in time with the orchestra of voices and clapping hands. Her skin was like the night, with beads of sweat glinting like stars in the light of the gods against her flawless midnight skin. She was perfect.

The moment had come. The pace of the singing slowed and the clapping stopped. The married women came forth with wooden bowls filled with water, and the married men brought forth with small bundles of sticks and grass bearing a fire blessed by the three elders. The unmarried women took the water, and the unmarried men took the fire. It was time to choose. We sang to them, each asking to be chosen:

> *Beloved I beg you choose me! Dance I will dance!*
> *Offer your water to me! Dance I will dance!*
>
> *I'll kick up the dust for you! Dance I will dance!*
> *Tell me what I must do! Dance I will dance!*
>
> *Hear the elders singing! Dance I will dance!*
> *This is only the beginning! Dance I will dance!*
>
> *Say you'll me my wife! Dance I will dance!*
> *Together we will make a life! Dance I will dance...*

We danced again. Holding the fire and water above our heads, whirling in a circle like the wind in a storm. We shuffled, back and forth, mixing in amongst each other and then retreating to our lines. The clapping stopped, and it was time to choose. Each of the unmarried women came forth in a line and knelt before the man they would take as their husband. Yahuia knelt before me and offered her bowl. I turned my fire into the water and with a hiss it died. I had accepted. I touched her head. A great crescendo of clapping and ululations celebrated the new unions. Yahuia stood before me, her eyes overflowing with ardour. I turned to look at my brother. There was no bowl for his fire, it still burned.

I looked to A'azgimai, who poured her water into the dirt and retreated to the crowd. As the crowd closed in on us, I spied Izkah slipping away. I called to him, but he did not hear me, and I could not leave.

The singing and celebrating went long into the night, all of the happy couples sat together and watched as the children of our village bounced happily before us around the great bonfire, signs of what was to come for us in the future. Dawish had found a wife in Layla. She seemed to have looked past his terrible dancing. Izkah however, was nowhere to be found. The day had long gone and still he was nowhere to be seen.

I stared into the fire. "I should go and look for him, he must be so embarrassed."

"Stay with me beloved." She wrapped herself around my arm. "Give him time, he will come back. He has to stand for you at the wedding does he not?"

I smiled. "He does."

We stayed there at the fire, warmed by the flames and each other. We ate well. My grandfather had seen to it. Crabs and roasted plantains, fruit, and honey combs filled our bellies.

The elders gave grand speeches about love and marriage, raising children and loving the gods. Elder Jahi waved his cane about and told parents that they were the law, that they must ensure that there is order and discipline in the home, that they must remember the gods always. Elder Rahmi spoke of balance, stressing that even handedness must be the order of the day. Neither man nor woman was superior in the home, only that they were different parts to the structure that set the foundations for a family. Elder Rahi stressed tenderness. We must love and preserve each other. We must never allow any conflict to break our unions apart. We must be loyal and kind to one another.

One by one, the married men and women of the village stood in front of us and swore that they would always be there to support us should we experience trouble in our home. They offered to stand for us and help us stay together and happy. I looked at Yahuia, and I knew that the rest of my life was set. I kissed her tenderly on the forehead and we sat together looking into the fire as if it showed us visions of all the years to come.

Three days had passed since the ceremony. Each morning Yahuia would come to meet me and we would share breakfast together. She would come and rouse me from my bed and we would eat and talk. After breakfast, we would go and help the village build the marital huts for ourselves and all of the new couples. Though Sun may have been in the sky already, my day had no light before Yahuia greeted me with her smile. This morning, she did not come, and I had not seen her all day. I was worried.

"Where is my Yahuia?" I asked my father.

He looked at me smiling. "You miss her one morning, and now seek her so ardently? Soon she will be at your side every day."

"I have not seen her all day. Father, you know that we have breakfast together every morning." I replied.

"I have not seen her, Imsaid." He bit into a wedge of pomegranate and shook his head. "Go and find your betrothed. Just remember, fire that burns too hot burns out quickly."

Since Yahuia chose me, my father had become softer with me. Seeing that a woman thought enough of me to make me her husband seemed to have earned me more respect from him. He no longer tried to humiliate me with extra work or discipline me like a child. He spoke to me kindly and gave me advice. I was no longer an unruly boy to him, I was man, and one that he wanted to see flourish.

Izkah, on the other hand had been gone for three days. He was known for his constitutionals, but they normally never lasted more than a day. The grasses beyond our village were full of dangerous whooping hyenas and lions with shoulders taller than a man. The gods protected us by the sea, but out there was a different place. None ever went that far out. So many days gone made me wonder if the one who shared my divine fire was burning different coals. Not being chosen at the ceremony wounded him more deeply than I could have ever known.

"Where is my Yahuia?" I asked Yunus as he emerged from his hut.

"She is probably in her future sibling's birth hut. She has been fussing over it for days," He replied. "Seek her there."

He spoke the truth. When the day's work was done and supper had been eaten, Yahuia would head straight for the hut we built. She would stay up late many a night trying to make it perfect. Now that she was to be a married woman, it was all the more important for her to get this right as a parting gift to her parents before she and I moved in to our own home.

I followed his suggestion and walked to the rear of his hut where the new construction had been built.

"Yahuia?" I called. "Yahuia?"

Silence, no… breathing, no… sobbing.

I followed the sound to the hut and pulled the wildebeest skin away from the door. There was Yahuia, sitting with her back against the wall and her knees to her chest, hanging her head and weeping.

"Yahuia!"

She looked up at me, and her weeping intensified. I ran to her and tried to embrace her, to kiss away her tears and comfort her. She rebuffed me with an extended arm.

"No!" She forced between her sobs. "No!"

"What happened? Please! Tell me!" I fell to my knees before her. "Have I done something?"

She shook her head.

"Has someone hurt you?"

She did not answer.

"Yahuia! Who has hurt you? Tell me so that I can bring it to the elders. Tell me what happened!"

She looked at me, her eyes red and sorrowful. "Ask your brother."

My heart skipped. It all came together. The looks, the silence, the distance, and now this.

"What did Izkah do to you?" My hands were trembling.

"I can't." She sobbed and shook her head. "I can't"

I sat close to her and kissed her hand. "I swear to you Yahuia, whatever has happened, whatever it is, I promise that you will be blameless. Tell me what has happened."

She remained silent.

"Look at me." I tilted her head so that she could see my eyes. "Look at me. You are safe here with me. Tell me what has happened so that I may set it right."

"Do you swear to the gods and on the heads of our ancestors that you will keep the peace, no matter what I tell you?"

I kissed my fingers and touched my heart, the seat of my divine fire.

"Last night I was here preparing the hut for my mother and Izkah came to see me." She sniffled. I wiped away a tear with my thumb. "He returned from his long walk and it seemed that he was here to make amends. He offered me a pomegranate as a peace offering. He cut it open and gave me a wedge. When I ate it, something happened, and when I came to my senses..." The tears came again, she began to quiver.

"Hush, hush." I pulled her close to me and put her head on my chest. "What happened?"

She forced the words out between her tears, and what she said next hit me like a tidal wave.

"He was on top of me, inside of me. I told him to get off but he told me that I swore to love him, that I would marry him, that I wanted him. I couldn't stop him. When he finished, I lashed at him with the rope and told him to leave. His eyes...his eyes were not the same. He ran into the night and left me here."

A fire burned inside of me that I never imagined was possible. I held her tight to me and let her cry; my lips spoke comfort through the tender kisses I laid upon her forehead. Inside I was seething, hotter than the molten rock vomiting from Sunshadeen's Mouth. Izkah must be punished.

"I need you to come with me." I said as tenderly as my rage would allow. "Izkah cannot be allowed to do this to you and go unpunished."

"No." she said weakly. "No."

She was afraid.

I took her hand into mine and stood tall. "I will keep you safe. No angry hand shall touch you so long as I am with you. Come and let us find you justice."

She looked up at me with those pools of splendour and rose to her feet. She embraced me. I held her and waited until she was ready to let go, though I wished that she never would. When she was ready, she looked me in the eye and nodded. I lead her by the wrist to the site of our marital hut and where our families were hard at work and sought my brother out.

"Izkah!" I shouted. "IZKAH! IZKAAAAAH!"

"Imsaid, what is wrong with you?" My father came up to me with is clay-caked arms outstretched, gesturing for me to calm down. "What vexes you so my son, why do you shout?"

My mother and Yahuia's mother got up from braiding rope and came to us. "What is wrong with Yahuia?" My mother asked.

"Ask my brother." I said, the fire in me rising. "IZKAAAAAAAH!"

The village began to gather, and then I saw him, slinking away from the growing crowd.

"IZKAH!" I shouted. My feet took flight and I ran him down.

He tried to run, but his leg was still sore from the flogging Elder Jahi had given him several days ago. I caught him and by the shoulders I threw him up against the half-built structure, the still wet clay smacking against his back.

"WHY?" I shouted into his face. "WHY?"

"I don't know what you are talking about." Izkah protested. "Why are you so angry?"

"Imsaid, you have gone mad, why are you attacking your brother?" Elder Rahi's tremulous voice demanded an answer. "What is wrong with you?"

"Ask Izkah, O grandfather!" I shouted. "Tell them what you did to Yahuia!"

"I don't..."

I slapped him. "NO LIES! TELL THEM WHAT YOU..."

His eyes were different, Yahuia was right. They were empty, I did not see the divine fire we shared burning in them anymore. The world went quiet. My belly was wet. I stepped back from him. My head felt light, I looked at my hand, and it was red. His hand was red, his knife was red.

"..did." the world shrank into blackness, and Yahuia's voice faded into the distance.

She said my name, she loved me. I loved her. Her smile was the beauty of all creation. She was light, she was life, and she was my beloved. Nothing in my life could rival her beauty. Her midnight hair curled like the waves of the sea, her skin was flawless onyx, and her eyes were deep pools of splendour that begged me to drown each time I beheld them. O Yahuia! She was my one desire, and for her love I would have died a thousand deaths.

Izkah's Desire

I do not know by what power the gods made her, but she was the embodiment of perfection. She was the culmination of all of my desires moulded into a star that walked among men. I would never have the words or confidence to confess my heart to her. She never saw me, even when she looked into my eyes while I was lost in hers. I thought that she could love me once, I was sure of it. I was clever enough to design stronger huts. I was smart enough to show the men how to carry ostrich eggs full of water on a hunt. I was inquisitive enough ask the questions that needed to be asked. I was brave enough to learn the things that we did not know, even when others did not care to investigate. For all of my qualities, I could not think of a way to make her love me.

My brother was one among the few who understood me. He never made me feel like an outcast. Elder Rahi would say that given the fact that we were twins, Imsaid and I shared a divine fire. It seemed that we burned on different kindling. He was gregarious and witty. He was troublesome yet loveable. I remember once when we were children, Imsaid cut a hot pepper and squeezed the juice into our father's mouth while he napped. My father would have beaten him, but the idiot pretended to cry and rubbed his hand, wet with the pepper juice into his own eye and punished himself. He was foolish, but he was my brother, and I loved him well.

The people loved him well, but they never showed me the same affection. Elder Jahi never spared me a caning when he saw fit, and my father was always short with me. I would sometimes hear them whisper that I was strange. They would enjoy the fruit of my ingenuity, but always looked on me as though I had the head of a snake.

Our home was by the endless water, which reflected the sky above us, bright when the gods were happy and terrible when they were not. I never understood the gods, their intentions were never clear. They gave us so much, and yet it still never seemed to be enough. They never gave me what I wanted.

Imsaid and I were met by the object of my desire on the way to help her parents build a hut for her yet unborn sibling. The smile that shone between her lips was the ivory glory of the moon in its fullness. For a brief moment, I forgot the soreness of my thigh left behind by Elder Jahi's cane.

"Izkah! Imsaid!" Her arms outstretched.

"Yahuia!" We said in unison.

She embraced us together. I wished that I could have kept that embrace to myself, but as with many things, I had to share it with my brother.

"You heard the news! I am going to be an elder sister!" She was so full of happiness. "I hope this time it is a girl. My parents produce nothing but boys." She winked at me. "Not that there is anything wrong with that. Come! My father needs help collecting clay for the walls and palm leaves for the roof."

"Another baby." Imsaid said. "Do your parents know when to quit?"

My brother was such an idiot sometimes. Yunus and Yara had many children over the years, but only Yahuia managed to live beyond her fifth year. Many of them died in the womb and never broke water. "Imsaid…"

"Izkah, what happened to your leg?" Yahuia had noticed the change in my gait and poked at my thigh. I tried not to wince.

"Elder Jahi" we said in unison again.

"You asked him something silly again didn't you?" Yahuia shook her head. "Izkah when will you ever learn?"

I lifted my head and with pride I answered. "That is exactly what I want to do Yahuia, I want to learn. There are so many things that we do not know. Why does Sun cross the sky? Why does Sunshaia weep to send us water from that same sky? Why can we drink from the river and not the sea? I want to know things; I want to know the world for more than what we see on the surface. And every lump that I earn in that quest is worth the exchange."

"Try to avoid getting too many more lumps. The Choosing Ceremony is coming soon and I would not want for you to damage that handsome face and ruin your prospects for a wife." She caressed my face with her finger and left to return to her work making bark rope.

"She said I was handsome." My brother was delusional.

"She was taking to me Imsaid." I was handsome to her eye, we looked the same, but it was me she called handsome.

"Well you are an uglier version of me, so if she calls you handsome, then it means I am even more handsome than that."

"Sometimes I wonder about you. How is your head so empty?"

"Izkah, your leg is too tender to haul stones or tread clay. Go and make fibre for rope and I will help our father and the others with the clay and stone."

"I can still help." I stood up straight, not wanting to embarrass myself with the work of the elderly.

"Catch me then." Before I could answer, Imsaid tapped my sore thigh and ran off like a fool. My knee nearly buckled.

"Fine! I will braid rope!" Giving chase was not worth the energy.

When I finally made it to the village, I found the people there singing and working. The healthiest men walked back and forth carrying bundles of clay and piling it near Yunus and Yara's marital hut while others dug the foundations and planted the stakes. Some of the older men sat near the women, stripping and beating bark until the fibres were soft enough to braid. The women, with quick and nimble fingers crafted fine and strong rope as quickly and expertly as they braided each other's hair.

I greeted A'azgimai and Layla, who simply looked at me and returned to their work. They had spoken about me, I was sure of it, but what they said, that was between them and the gods. I took up a seat next to Yahuia and in an effort to preserve my masculinity, set to pounding the bark as I listened to the people work and sing. The people sang for everything. From Sun's rising until well after the sky was painted at the end of the day. For them, singing was as natural as the beating of the heart. I was never one for singing, but I did love to listen. Yahuia sang loudly along with the people.

Beloved I beg you choose me! Dance I will dance!
Offer your water to me! Dance I will dance!

I'll kick up the dust for you! Dance I will dance!
Tell me what I must do! Dance I will dance!

Hear the elders singing! Dance I will dance!
This is only the beginning! Dance I will dance!

Say you'll me my wife! Dance I will dance!
Together we will make a life! Dance I will dance…

"I see you are excited to become an elder sister." I tried to strike up a conversation.

She smiled in the way that she does, the way that makes my knees weaker than any blow from Elder Jahi's cane. "My parents have been trying to give me a brother or sister for years."

"What about having your own? You are old enough to choose this year." I kept my eyes trained on my task, trying to avoid her reaction.

She stopped braiding for a moment, seemingly lost in thought. Her smile remained. "I am."

I had opened the door; I might as well walk through it. "Have you given any thought to whom you might choose?"

She nudged me with her shoulder. "You know I am not supposed to tell you that, it would curse the union. If I make a choice, I want the gods to sow great favour upon it. I want to be with a man that loves and cherishes me. I want the right man to put his fire in my water."

"There are many hoping to make you their wife." I half mumbled my eyes still on the bark fibres as I pulled them apart.

"I am sure that there are many women that would want to be with you, Izkah." She changed the subject. "You are by far one of the most intelligent men in the village. Look at all the things you think up. Any woman would be lucky to have you."

I smiled shyly "Any man would be lucky to have you."

A'azgimai and Layla snickered at me. I shot them a look. Layla went back to braiding, but A'azgimai stuck out her tongue, and then returned to work.

Something caught Yahuia's eye in the distance. "And here we are, two lucky charms."

I tried to spy the thing that so quickly seized her attention, but it was gone by the time I noticed she was watching.

She picked up another bundle of loose fibre and began to braid it. "Has your brother given any indication at who he might want to choose him?"

"I never asked him. He didn't seem too concerned with the ceremony." I lowered my voice "Though I think that A'azgimai might have an eye for him, and you know her, she always gets what she wants."

"She does." Yahuia nodded. "My cousin has a very strong will. My father says that she is more Sunshadeen than Sunshaia."

A'azgimai was strong willed, and strong of arm as well. Some time ago she was out on the water, and single-handedly dragged a fish out of the deep that would have pulled most to their deaths.

"You would know what she wants better than I, perhaps you should ask her." I suggested.

Yahuia nodded. "Maybe it is you she has an eye for. You and Imsaid do look alike."

"But I am the handsome one." I quipped. "You said so yourself."

She laughed as she coiled a length of rope and added it to the pile of wound and bound rope she and other women had spun together. We continued making rope and chatting between singing. The day had gone so fast that we did not even notice it was ending.

"Enough, enough!" Elder Rahi clapped his hands. "Sun is about to paint the sky, it is time to pay homage and prepare our dinner!

I have been smoking fish all day, and I am sure you are all very hungry."

My great-grandfather was always so kind. He was the softest hand of the three elders, and was always busying himself with making sure everyone ate, and that we were all well. He was one with a remarkable healing hand. There was not a child in this village who I know of who had not been blessed by his hand within minutes of being born. He often said of my twin brother and I that we shared a divine fire, and that made our bond as brothers unique. He was me and I was him, or we were at least different halves of the same person. I was never sure. It was eerie to me sometimes to look into his face and see myself so clearly.

"Come on Izkah, let us go and help prepare the meal." Yahuia pulled me up by the arm. "Unless your leg is too sore to carry a basket of fish."

I rolled my eyes and stood up to follow her to collect the fish. On the way to Elder Rahi's smoking hut, I saw my father and the other men from the clay pit. Imsaid was not among them.

"Father! Where is Imsaid?" I asked. "Should he not be among you?"

"Your bother is hauling stones, penance for skylarking whilst the rest of us worked." He replied before pouring water from a water skin I made over his body, washing away the red clay that caked his ebony skin. "Give him a little longer and then seek him out. Ten more stones and he can join us."

The evening wore on. Sun had begun to paint the sky and Elder Rahi was going to sing the Song of Creation. The smoked fish hung on a rack over the fire in the centre of the village, my mouth salivated as the smell of our warming meal tickled my nostrils. It was flavoured with salt wrought from the endless waters and basted in honey, monitored attentively by Elders Rahi and Rahmi.

"I should go and get Imsaid." I said. "It is almost time to eat."

I stood up to go find him; Yahuia stood up before me and put a hand on my shoulder. "Do not trouble yourself. Your thigh is still sore. I will go and collect him. Just wait here and save us some leaves."

Who was I to argue with her? Her touch was enough to make me say 'yes'. I nodded and obeyed, returning to my seat. Elder Rahi began to sing, his voice was true. He sang and clapped his hands. He wove within the melody the tale of how Sun, Sunshadeen, and Sunshaia conspired to create the world.

Sun split into two, Sunshadeen, a faceless man wreathed in fire, and Sunshaia, a faceless woman formed in water. She clapped her hands and brought forth the waters of the world. She then kissed the waves and gave rise to land. Sunshadeen brought light by striking his hands together and igniting Sun with his flames. Sunshaia then put her fingers into the earth and from it sprang all plant life. Sunshadeen took water from the sea and with Sunshaia formed man and animals, breathing his divine fire into each creature and granting it life. Each day, Sun would cross the sky and the gods would marvel at their creations. At night they gifted us the moon and stars to leave us awestruck by their beauty. When our time was done on this earth, Sunshadeen would return to claim the divine fire he breathed into us and return it to Sun's great halo.

Elder Rahi also sang of the Sunbaka, a darkness that the gods have kept from us, one they have put to sleep in a place that we cannot go. It was all the elders would tell us about it, and the fact that they jealously guarded that knowledge frustrated me to no end. What good is knowledge if not shared?

Yahuia had been away for some time. The banana leaves were being passed around to share the meal.

"Dawish, hold some leaves for Yahuia, Imsaid and I." I said to my cousin. "I will go and find them."

I stood up and left the centre of the village. I paced between the huts for a moment, and then decided to go look by the sea. Imsaid would likely have been bathing himself there and Yahuia would have been having a warm time coaxing him away from the waves. My brother loved the water. One would think he was part fish.

I made my way down to the shoreline, scanning the waters for a sign of Yahuia and Imsaid. I saw nothing. It was getting dark, and wild animals would soon come close to the village like they did every night. I walked towards the water, and then I heard something that sounded like moaning. My head swivelled from left to right, searching for the source of the sound. Then I saw them, coiled in each other's arms and swaying with the tide. Making love out of wedlock was no crime; however I could not help but feel that something had been stolen from me.

My heart shattered into a thousand pieces, ground further into dust with each thrust my brother pressed into her body. I hung my head, turned around and returned to the fire, pretending that I had not seen the woman I desired with every fibre of my being swathed in the arms of my very own brother.

They returned but did not sit beside me. Instead, they sat on opposite sides of the fire, stealing looks at one another as though we were all oblivious to the cause of their tardiness. I could not put words to the sensation that coursed through my body. I did not know whether to be angry, whether I should cry, or whether I should accept the fact that she did not love me. Perhaps there was still time for me to convince her that I was the better man. Not even the honey Elder Rahmi so lovingly spread over the fish could sweeten the bitterness on my tongue.

For several days after the incident, I withdrew myself. I did the minimum required to help build the hut. I did not remain with the people for long as they sang to celebrate completing the construction. Instead I retired to the hut my brother and I shared, which he seemed inclined to leave at odd times of the night when he thought I was sleeping. I knew where he was going. I knew what he was doing, and it was a knife in my heart every time.

Long days and sleepless nights all seemed to blend into one formless passage of time. Until Elder Rahmi blasted his ram's horn and roused us all from slumber, I had forgotten that the Choosing Ceremony had come upon us. My brother and I sprang up, washed our faces and quickly painted the flames of Sunshadeen on our bodies before donning our fibre cloaks and running to the village centre.

There all of the unmarried men and women were arrayed in their finery. The men stood proud and handsome in their grass and bark fibre cloaks and red body paint. The women were beautiful, standing bare breasted in their grass skirts, their skin painted with white swirls to honour the water goddess. The singing began and the ceremony was under way. We had to present ourselves to the girls first, dancing in such a way as to demonstrate our vitality.

Imsaid stepped forward first. He was a spectacular dancer, light as a blowing leaf and sure in his steps. He paraded in front of the girls as they clapped, flipping his cloak and bouncing like an antelope. The girls ululated in delight as he flirted with them, paying special attention to Yahuia. A'azgimai watched him as well. I suspected that she wanted him. She could have him. The image of Yahuia making love to my brother in the early twilight returned to my mind. I clenched my jaw and pushed it out. Yahuia had not chosen yet, perhaps I could change her mind. I continued clapping and singing with the rest, losing myself in the rhythm and preparing for my turn.

Next it was Dawish that threw himself into the space between our lines, spreading out his broad chest in an effort to tantalize the women. He was big and broad, powerful as a buffalo and about as intelligent as a rock. He was also as graceful as a khurt, thrashing about wildly and nearly losing his balance. The older women ululated as he continued his frenzied dance, flexing his muscles and nearly tripping on his cloak. He finally returned to the line, and it was my turn.

"Sunshaia make her see me." I appealed to the water goddess under my breath.

I broke from the line and began to dance. Though not as flamboyant as my brother, I was still a competent dancer. I danced harder than I had ever done anything in my life. My feet pounded the earth and I flipped my cloak, the sweat ran down my face and stung my eyes. Still I danced. I needed her to see me; I needed to show her that I was vital. I kicked my feet up and fell to my knees before her, looking up with pleading eyes. She did not see me. I retreated back to the line and melted into the chorus.

Other men from the village took their turn, spinning and jumping, flipping their cloaks and making their interest known to the women they fancied. Through it all I watched her, while she watched him, and he watched her. I had lost. The elders of the village came and brought bowls of water for the unmarried women and bundles of burning grass for the unmarried men. The time had come to choose. The song changed, and we sang to the women, pleading to be chosen:

Beloved I beg you choose me! Dance I will dance!
Offer your water to me! Dance I will dance!

I'll kick up the dust for you! Dance I will dance!
Tell me what I must do! Dance I will dance!

Hear the elders singing! Dance I will dance!
This is only the beginning! Dance I will dance!

Say you'll me my wife! Dance I will dance!
Together we will make a life! Dance I will dance…

I held my fire above my head, swaying side to side, and stepping in time with the others as we made our last ditch effort to show our worth. I watched Yahuia with eyes full of hope and dread. It was like watching my dreams drown and die. Imsaid extinguished his flame into her bowl and it was decided. Yahuia would marry my brother. I saw A'azgimai sport a look full of disappointment as she watched the pairing.

I looked at her. Our eyes met, and she tipped her bowl, draining out the water. My flame remained unquenched. I was not chosen. Even Dawish was chosen, I suppose Layla liked her men slow.

As the people crowded together to celebrate the new engagements, I smothered my fire in the dirt and took my leave. The woe of love that would go on unrequited poured from my eyes and ran down my face, turning red from the ochre that coloured the flames on my cheeks. I had no desire to celebrate the breaking of my heart. I could not bear to hear them singing, I could not bear their happiness when it was the cause of my sorrow.

I walked and I wept. I had no care for what hungry predator may be watching. It would have been better for them to take me. I had no will to live, though I was unsure if it was the loss of Yahuia or the sheer embarrassment of no offer of marriage that wounded me so. Either way, I kept walking. I walked until Sun began to paint the sky. My stomach grumbled with hunger and fortuitously, I came upon a pomegranate tree, branches hanging low with their fat red fruit. I pulled one from the tree and cut it open with my knife. The red juice ran down the flint blade and over my fingers. I ate of it, chewing he sour fruit and pieces of the bitter husk. Sunshaia gave us fruit. She made them of all kinds, from sweet mangos to sour lemons. Yahuia loved fruit; pomegranates were her favourite above all others. We never had them often, as it always meant a long walk from the village, longer than it took to get mangos, pears, or lemons.

Sunshaia could give us all of this fruit, all of these trees, all of this grass, and even mother's milk. She could give me a heart to love, but she could not give me the love of the heart that I craved. I threw the fruit away in frustration and threw my back against the tree. Tears came again, and I wept. I cursed the gods. I cursed Sun for making me see this day; I cursed Sunshadeen for not giving me the strength to overcome this pain, I cursed Sunshaia for making me want to love. In my agony, the gods were dead to me.

Night fell, and the hyenas began to whoop. The moon was full, and lit the Green Sea in a pale glow against the darkness. I climbed into the tree's higher branches to keep myself out of the reach and sight of any hungry predators that sought an easy meal. I wedged myself into the fork of a branch. I closed my eyes and leaned my head back. Sleep came.

"Izkah." An unfamiliar voice called my name.

I opened my eyes and looked around. "Who said that?"

My heart was a stampeding elephant. If we were the only people in the world, who could be calling my name?

"Izkah, why do you cry?"

A cold sensation ran down my spine. I pulled my cloak around my shoulders to ward off the chill. "Who are you?"

"A friend."

"If you are a friend, speak your name, let me see you." I swivelled my head, trying to connect a face to the voice. I saw nothing.

"I will do better than that." The voice whispered. "I will help you."

"How will you do that?"

"Extend your hand and I will show you."

Hesitantly, I obeyed, and as I extended my hand, a pomegranate dropped into my open palm.

"Your heart is broken, and the gods have abandoned you." The voice said. "I understand your pain, and if you will accept my friendship, I will give you what you most desire."

"Yahuia."

"Yes."

I felt something crawling up my leg. I looked down and jerked when I saw a cobra sliding against my skin. I reached for my knife, prepared to cut its head off before it bit me.

"Stay your hand Izkah." The voice said.

I uneasily took my hand away from my waistband and let the snake climb up my leg, around the branch and up my arm. It was heading for the fruit.

"Give to her this fruit and let her taste of it" the voice said as the cobra sank its fangs into the pomegranate I held, droplets of the crimson juice running from the corners of its mouth.

I watched the cobra draw its fangs from the fruit and retreat into the night "Why?"

"Give to her this fruit and let her taste of it. Her desire for you shall burn hotter than a thousand times one thousand Suns."

I was skeptical. "Why would you do this? What will you gain from it?"

"You have already given me a gift. I am only returning the favour."

I cradled the fruit in my hands, looking at the means by which I would have what my heart most desired. "How long will it last?"

"Forever, provided you abstain from entering her until you are wed." The voice began to fade. "Give to her this fruit, and she will be yours."

When Sun rose over the horizon, I climbed down from the tree, removed my cloak and filled it with pomegranates to bring home. I took special care to keep hers separate from the others. When I returned home, evening had fallen again, and I was greeted by my father.

"Izkah, where did you go?" he chided me. "Your mother was worried. If you were gone one more night we would have sent men to find you in the wilderness. Where did you go?"

Nothing I said would calm my father's storm. Instead, I presented him with my cloak full of pomegranates. "I needed to go for a walk. I walked a little too far, and decided not to come back empty handed. Please father, take as many as you like."

My father smiled at the offering and took for himself an armful. "This should be enough. Your mother will be happy to see the gift you have brought. Come home and rest your feet."

"By and by I will come, father. I want to share the pomegranates with some of the others."

My father smiled at me and nodded. "Good man. We have saved some food or you, it is waiting in my hut."

"Thank you father." I forced a smile and accepted a pat on the shoulder.

When we parted ways, I left the bundle of pomegranates in the village centre and sought Yahuia out. She would likely be at home, preparing the new hut for her unborn sibling.

The light of a small fire flickered from behind the wildebeest hide hanging from the top of the door. I closed my eyes, took a deep breath, and called to her.

"Yahuia."

"Yes."

"May I come in?"

She pushed the hide aside and poked her head out. "Izkah! Where did you go? No one has seen or heard from you since the ceremony."

"I-I needed to go for a walk. I brought you something" I produced the pomegranate.

"A pomegranate!" Her eyes lit up. "Where did you get this?"

"From a tree." I smiled.

She clicked her tongue and tried to snatch it. I pulled it away and drew my knife. "Let me cut it for you."

"Come in, I am just about finished preparing the hut. I am excited to show you what I have done."

I followed her back into the hut, cutting open the fruit, the red juice running down my knife and over my fingers as I cut.

"I finally finished preparing the straps for binding her feet and dug the pit for the birth string to be buried. I am waiting for my father to finish preparing the hides for the floor and I still need to weave a basket for him, or her, to sleep. I am sure that it is going to be a girl." She was giddy with excitement. I was so entranced by her presence I almost forgot what I was holding and took a bite myself. "Here, take your fruit."

"Do you not want any?" She accepted it with both hands.

"I have had plenty. If I eat any more I might swell up and turn red." I forced a chuckle. She bit into a wedge, crunching the seeds and swallowing the juice. Nothing seemed to change. I closed my eyes and sighed. "Yahuia, I need to tell you something."

"What?" She said between bites, already halfway through her second wedge.

"It's about your marriage to Imsaid."

"What marriage to Imsaid?" She looked up at me. "I am going to marry you."

I was stunned. "What?"

She finished the fruit and wiped the juice from her lips with the back of her hand. "I said I am going to marry you."

I could not believe it, how could this magic have worked so quickly? "You will?" I stepped towards her. "What about my brother?"

"I made a mistake, beloved." She threw the rind aside and reached out to me. "Forgive me. Tomorrow I will tell him and the elders that I have changed my decision. I want you."

I took her into my arms. "You want me?"

Her eyes drew me in the same way a pond draws stones to its bottom.

"I need you." She pulled me to her and kissed me.

Our embrace tightened, and our kiss intensified. I felt the rapid pace of her rampaging heart through my own chest, it only served to excite me further, then the voice echoed in my head. I was not to enter her until we wed or the spell would be broken.

"No." I stepped back. "Yahuia we should wait."

"Why? There is no law against it." She pulled me close again, pressing her breasts against my skin and reaching into my loincloth. "I want you now."

I succumbed to the screaming of my flesh and kissed her. We exposed our nakedness and made love on the floor of the hut. Her kisses were sweet, her caresses soft, her body a paradise. We swore love to one another as we neared our climax. Then, something changed.

"Izkah, what are you doing?" She said.

I pressed myself further into her. "Loving you, Yahuia. Tell me again that you want to marry me."

"No." Her voice was more urgent this time, her hands pushing me away instead of drawing me in. "Izkah, stop!"

"But you love me." I pushed harder. "You said that you loved me."

"No!" She dug her nails into my flesh; she drew blood from my shoulder. "Get off me!"

I withdrew myself and backed away. Her eyes were no longer overflowing with ardour, they were full of rage.

She whipped me with the rope. "GET OUT! GET OUT! GET OUUUUUUT!"

I ran out the door and into the night. I ran back to the hut my brother and I shared and I lay down and pretended to sleep. I lay there with my eyes closed until the morning came.

Before my brother woke, I slipped into the early light of the dawn to join the rest of the village as they built the marriage huts for the new couples. I busied myself with stacking the stones between the gaps in the frame and packing them with mud. Yahuia would say nothing. She chose to make love to me. I said no first. She changed her mind. I did not force her.

"IZKAH!" I knew that voice, and my heart thumped at the anger in its tone.

I peeked from behind the wall and saw Imsaid marching in my direction through the people, pulling Yahuia by the wrist. No good would come of speaking with him now. I tried to remove myself from his reach, but he found me. I tried to outrun him, but my sore leg would not give me the speed I needed. He grabbed me and threw me against the wet clay of the half-constructed wall.

"WHY?" He spat at me in a rage. "WHY?"

"I don't know what you are talking about." I pretended ignorance. "Why are you so angry?"

"Imsaid, you have gone mad, why are you attacking your brother?" Elder Rahi was wroth with the disturbance. "What is wrong with you?"

"Ask Izkah, O grandfather!" He shouted. "Tell them what you did to Yahuia!"

"I don't..."

He struck me so hard across the head my ears rang. "NO LIES!"

"Defend yourself, my friend." The voice had returned. "Defend yourself."

"TELL THEM WHAT YOU..." the fire suddenly left my brother's eyes. "...did."

He collapsed as a river of red flowed forth from his quivering body. My trembling hand dripped with his life force, wet from that same river.

"NOOOOO!" Yahuia screamed, running to kneel at his side.

The moment was surreal. I felt as though I had exited my body and watched someone else stab Imsaid in the belly. Someone else sent half of my divine fire back to Sun's halo. In an instant, Dawish and others of my kin descended upon me, wrested the implement of my crime from my hand and dragged me limp into a hut where they threw me down and blocked the door. I was a prisoner.

I lay there on my back, looking at the blood, now caked dry into a black layer of flaking scales from my fingertips to my elbow. I had killed my brother. I had broken the peace and killed him. Never in the memory of the people had anyone ever committed such an unconscionable act. It had to be me, and my brother had to be the first one. Tears came to me as the weight of my misdeed bore down upon my breast. I curled my knees to my chest and bawled until exhaustion overtook me and gave me to slumber.

"Izkah!"

I opened my eyes to my father's silhouette in the doorway. "Father?"

"What have you done, Izkah?" He asked with a low growl. "Why?"

"I am sorry." I wept again. "The gods only know why I killed him. I never wanted...I never wanted to take his life. He yelled at me, he hit me and I..."

"I told you to wait until she wed you." The voice was not my father's.

Before I could utter another word, the silhouette that I thought was my father's descended upon me, scaly hands around my throat and squeezing the divine fire out of me. I could not fight, I was too weak. I thrashed my arms but it was to no avail. I closed my eyes and gave in to the darkness.

"Izkah!"

My eyes opened and I sat up, my arms still reaching out to fight an assailant that only existed in my guilty nightmare. I rubbed what little sleep I had from my eyes and blinked in the blinding light of the late morning.

"Get up. The elders summon you."

"Good morning, Dawish." I rose to my feet and dusted the dirt from my legs. "Did you bring water?"

He grabbed my arm, his fingers dug into my flesh. "I said the elders have summoned you."

I took that as a sign that I would find no warmth at the feet of our patriarchs. Dawish dragged me through the village with his brothers in tow. The village gathered behind us, their faces full of fear, sorrow, and anger. Not a tongue wagged in my direction. Their eyes spoke loudly enough. They were taking me to Elder Jahi's hut. This would not be pleasant.

Dawish thrust me through the open doorway. I fell on my knees before the elders, who sat above me on their stools, the symbols of their authority. They looked on me with blank expressions. Only the gods knew what they felt.

"You know why you are here." Elder Rahmi began. "You violated my granddaughter, and you killed your brother."

I bowed my head. "I am so so-" My words were cut off by the crack of a cane across my back.

"You will shut your mouth, Izkah. Your words are empty." Elder Jahi scowled, striking me again before he returned to his seat.

"You are here, O grandson of mine, for us to decide what is to be done with you." My grandfather's voice trembled with sorrow.

I remained silent and kept my head low. I was at their mercy.

"Why did you do this? What drove you to attack my Yahuia?" Elder Rahmi asked; his voice was void of emotion.

I did not answer.

Elder Jahi's cane came down on me again. "Answer him!"

Elder Rahi raised his hand. "Jahi, be not so free with your cane. Your wroth is just, but you must spare the rod and his back. Breaking either of them will do us no favours. Speak up, Izkah."

"She was promised to me." I replied.

Elder Rahmi furrowed his brow and crossed his arms. "By whom? She chose Imsaid at the ceremony, Imsaid. You had no more rights to her than you do the tide."

I sighed. With nothing left to lose, I told them the story of the pomegranate tree, and the voice that promised me her love in exchange for a favour I had done.

Elder Rahi leaned forward. "What favour was that?"

I did not answer.

"Speak!" Elder Jahi stomped his foot.

"I do not know. He simply said that I had done him a favour and he was returning it. "I raised my eyes slightly to see the elders whispering amongst each other. Even the stoic Elder Rahmi had a look of distress on his face.

"Tell us more about this voice." Elder Rahmi leaned forward.

"I have told you all that I know."

The elders rose from their stools and huddled in a corner of the hut, speaking too low for me to hear. After a time, they returned to their seats and Elder Rahi spoke.

"My grandson, we are divided as to what is to be done with you. Jahi believes that the only punishment for your crime is death. He believes the injuries we do to others must be repaid in kind, and the injury you have caused is most grievous. Rahmi believes that you should be banished. The voice that spoke such evil into you must not be fed with blood, but he also believes that you cannot live among us after what you have done. I, on the other hand, likely blinded by my love for you, think you can be redeemed. The great strength of our people is our unity. That unity was broken, and darkness was fed by it. The only way to stem that evil is to love each other back into peace and harmony. The final decision, however, does not rest on our individual convictions. The people must be considered." Elder Rahi stood up, the other elders followed suit. "You will be confined to your hut until a decision is made."

"Dawish, take him away." Elder Jahi waved his cane.

My cousin did as he was told and dragged me back to my hut, again throwing me to the ground. They blocked the door and windows, and there I waited, slowly sinking into madness trying to determine which direction the people would take. Were it not for the leaf-wrapped meals my mother slid under the door for me, the darkness of my captivity would have me lose count of the days. There were three. They had been deliberating for three days and had not reached a decision. I wondered if killing me was still an option. Who would do it? What would be done with he that kills me? Do they reward him, or banish him? Perhaps he would be executed and the cycle should continue until there was no one left. I almost wanted to kill myself and save them the argument. It must be tearing them apart.

"Izkah."

"Leave me alone!" I said to the darkness, half-drunk with sleep.

"All of this is your fault, you did this to us!"

A pair of strong hands found their way around my throat and squeezed. This was no dream, this was my punishment. I writhed and kicked and thrashed, trying to free myself from the death grip that had seized me. My chest burned for air, but none came. My mind was screaming, though my mouth could not. I grew weary, my limbs fell limp.

"Dawish, hurry up before they see us!" A'azgimai rasped.

"I am almost done." He replied as he shook the final embers of divine fire from my body.

Yahuia's Desire

I loved him. His heart was kind and his eyes were playful. He was sweet, and his tongue was quick. His laughter was music to me. I loved to watch him run along the shoreline with his brother. The light of the gods made his flawless earthen skin glow like polished wood of ebon. I would fill my eyes with the sight of him kicking up sand in his wake near the endless glistening waters. O beloved!

I would lay in your arms 'till Sun tires of crossing the sky, and even then I would hold you still in the darkness.

I looked at him and wondered how a man could be so perfect, and then I would look at his brother and wonder how they could be so different. Imsaid was jovial, playful, and the lustre of his smile put the brightest pearls to shame. His twin brother, Izkah, was moody, awkward, and often tried to pry his way into things that were not his to know. Elder Jahi was always very hard on him. Despite his intelligence, he could be a nuisance with all of his questions. The gods gave us everything we could want and more. We never wanted for food and the skies were always beautiful, even when it rained. The water from the river was cool and clear, and always full of fish. All of this bounty never satisfied him.

I was happy with all that I had. My parents loved me, and I loved them dearly. The people of our village enjoyed a sacred peace that unified us and pleased the gods. I had my friends, my kin, and the bounty that the gods gifted unto us. This bounty grew ever greater when my parents announced that I was to become an elder sister.

"NO!" I put my hands over my smiling mouth, my eyes wide as the moon.

My mother nodded and smiled. I took her hands into mine and gripped them tightly. I looked to my father, who was standing above us, grinning like a monkey.

"Yes my Yahuia, it is true. The gods knew that you would soon leave us, and have decided to gift us with another child."

"I am going to be an elder sister again?" I half asked and half exclaimed. "I am going to be an elder sister!"

My mother nodded again and pulled me closer that I might embrace her. I wrapped my arms around her and squeezed. For years since my birth they had tried to give me a sibling, to grow our house. My mother would become with child, but Sunshadeen would not grant the unborn with a divine fire, and so my brother or sister would be lost. Sometimes the child would break water, but would fall to sickness or misfortune. Six times since I was a child they began to build birthing huts for my unborn siblings. Thrice the children were lost before the first rope was tied. Once my brother broke water, and

Sunshadeen had given him no divine fire. The only two that did survive birth died of fever before the age of five. We always tore huts down when the children died. The reminder their parting was too much to bear.

The gods were with them this time. Elder Rahi's hand was gifted in the ways of new life, and he gave his blessing for them to start building. My grandfather was ecstatic. Elder Rahmi would always complain that there were not enough babies in the village. He nearly danced on the spot when my mother broke the news to him. Life was always welcome among us. The gods are good to those who create and preserve it.

"Have you told the others yet?" I asked, my arms still around my mother.

"The elder women know, and your father will call up the men of the village start construction. There is plenty of work to do." She replied.

I knelt next my mother on the furs that covered the floor of their hut. "And we will all put our hands in to build, it is our way."

I offered my hands to her and we both rose to our feet. When we stepped out of my parents' hut, the people had already assembled. The men came with their tools in tow, and the women were already carrying bundles of bark to make rope. News travelled fast among the people, usually on the tongues of the elder women, and I was always the last to hear it.

They began to sing, striking up a chorus of clapping hands, ululations and dulcet tones. Without hesitation I joined in, holding my mother's hand aloft and dancing from side to side as we separated and went about our tasks. Making the rope would be the work of the women, children, and the elderly. Collecting the wood, clay, and stones to build the structure would be left to the healthy men. It was hard work, but to Izkah's credit, his idea of embedding large stones into the clay that made our walls strengthened our huts, allowing us to make them taller.

My mother went to sit with the married women, who fawned over her, bringing her water and telling her to rest. Her belly had not even grown as of yet. I smiled and rolled my eyes.

"Yahuia!"

I looked around for the voice.

"Yahuia! Get over here and help." A'azgimai waved to me from the village centre, sitting with Layla near a pile of bark fibre.

I walked to them, and listed to the rhythm of the elder men beating the bark into fibres with their stones while they sang of the Choosing Ceremony.

> *Beloved I beg you choose me! Dance I will dance!*
> *Offer your water to me! Dance I will dance!*
>
> *I'll kick up the dust for you! Dance I will dance!*
> *Tell me what I must do! Dance I will dance!*
>
> *Hear the elders singing! Dance I will dance!*
> *This is only the beginning! Dance I will dance!*
>
> *Say you'll me my wife! Dance I will dance!*
> *Together we will make a life! Dance I will dance…*

"Peace and blessings, Yahuia!" Layla welcomed me with an embrace.

"To you as well, Layla." I sat next to her, took a handful of fibre and started braiding.

"It seems that the Choosing Ceremony is on everyone's mind." A'azgimai remarked.

"It is only days away." Layla smiled. "Everyone had started to make their choices and the men are restless."

"Would you not be unsettled if you had to wait for someone to choose you, no matter how badly you wanted them?" I replied. "How embarrassing would it be to not be chosen at all? They have every right to be restless."

"You speak as though choosing is any easier than being chosen." A'azgimai replied, sorting through another bundle of fibre to add to her length of rope. "Have you met the men in this village?"

"What do you mean by that?" Layla tilted her head to the side with interest.

A'azgimai threw a look back at her. "I can count on one hand the number of men in this village that aren't completely useless."

"Give us the names of these men." I nudged her with my shoulder. "Who do you think the best prospects are?"

"And why would I tell you that?" A'azgimai smirked. "You might offer them your water and leave me without one to choose."

"I doubt that you and I have the same taste in men." Layla replied. "You will get no competition from me."

I cast a playfully suspicious eye on her. "It seems you have already chosen yours."

"You know I couldn't tell you my choice even if I had made it. It's bad luck." She winked at me. "All I can say is that I want someone that is tall, and has a very strong back."

"So...Dawish then." Said A'azgimai, her eyes still fixed on her hands as they braided.

Layla raised her eyebrows. "What makes you think that I chose him?"

A'azgimai kept her eyes on her work. "I saw, well I saw and heard you getting well acquainted with the strength in my brother's back behind a bush the other day. I am pretty sure the rest of the village heard you too. Things that have been seen cannot be unseen."

"Well at least I know my decision will be a good one." Layla tried to smile through her embarrassment. "We are going to be sisters."

"Lovely."

We marinated for a moment in the awkwardness of A'azgimai's revelation, braiding as we sang along with the elders.

"A'azgimai."

"Yes Yahuia."

"Have you caught any more monster fish lately?" I was terrible at changing subjects.

"No. There are plenty of fish in the water, but no monsters like the one I caught last dry season." She replied. "The biggest fish are not just difficult to catch, they are difficult to find. Sometimes they go fishing for you."

I had tried fishing once with a harpoon in the shallows. I was terrible at it. I kicked up too much sand and scared the fish away. When I had mastered not scaring the fish away, I forgot about the other creatures living in the endless waters, and was reminded of their existence when a crab pinched my toe. That put an end to my ambition of catching a great fish like A'azgimai. I remember the look of pride on her face juxtaposed to the look of astonishment on the faces of the men as she dragged a fish nearly the size of a man up the beach, her broken harpoon in its side. No one had ever caught a fish so large before or since. Many have tried, and they either drowned or returned empty handed, then again, A'azgimai was one of those women that always got what she wanted, not even the sea could deny her.

"Look, here come a pair of stragglers." A'azgimai pointed past me.

My gaze followed her finger, and at the end of it I saw two of my favourite people: Imsaid and his brother Izkah. They were a handsome pair. Elder Rahi often said that when twins were born, Sunshadeen split one divine fire and shared it between them. True their bond was special, but I had never seen two people that looked so alike and acted so differently. Truly I loved them both, but I was in love with Imsaid.

"It looks like Izkah ran afoul of Elder Jahi again. Watch his limp." Layla said.

"Why can't he be more like his bother?" A'azgimai shook her head. "Imsaid at least has a sense of humour to go with his good looks."

"I will be right back." I dropped my half-braided rope and stood up.

"Don't tarry too long." Layla waved her half-braided rope in my general direction.

I didn't reply. I trotted over to the twins with my arms outstretched. "Izkah! Imsaid!"

"Yahuia!" They said in unison. It always sounded like a song when they did that.

I embraced the both of them. They had been my playmates since we were all small children crawling at our mothers' feet. The sight of them always made me smile. I pressed my cheek against Imsaid's. He smelled like the sea.

"You heard the news! I am going to be an elder sister again!" I exclaimed. "I hope this time it is a girl. My parents produce nothing but boys." I winked at them. "Not that there is anything wrong with that. Come! My father needs help collecting clay for the walls and palm leaves for the roof."

"Another baby." Imsaid jested. "Do your parents know when to quit?"

I snickered to hide my discomfort. Imsaid meant no offence, but sometimes his tongue was faster than his good sense.

Izkah rolled his eyes. "Imsaid..."

"Izkah, what happened to your leg?" I poked at his thigh in an attempt to change the subject and ask about his limp.

"Elder Jahi" They said in unison again.

"You asked him something silly again didn't you?" I shook my head. "Izkah, when will you ever learn?"

He lifted his head in that way he always did when he pontificated. "That is exactly what I want to do Yahuia, I want to learn. There are so many things that we do not know. Why does Sun cross the sky? Why does Sunshaia weep to send us water from that same sky? Why can we drink from the river and not the sea? I want to know things; I want to know the world for more than what we see on the surface. And every lump that I earn in that quest is worth the exchange."

"Try to avoid getting too many more lumps. The Choosing Ceremony is coming soon and I would not want for you to damage that handsome face and ruin your prospects for a wife." I poked at his cheek and returned to my work. He was as handsome as his brother.

A'azgimai handed me the rope I had been braiding and a handful of fibre. "It looks like you are being followed."

I turned my head to see Izkah limping in our direction.

"Elder Jahi gave him another flogging for asking too many questions." I replied. "Watch his gait."

Layla and A'azgimai chuckled. They were well aware of Izkah's constant search for knowledge, even though there are some questions that should remain unasked.

"I hope he doesn't intend on braiding rope." Layla tied off a finished length of rope. "A'azgimai, pass some stones and bark for him and put them over there."

A'azgimai quickly grabbed a large and small stone and a handful of bark. When he arrived, he greeted A'azgimai and Layla. They looked him up and down and returned to their work. Izkah collected the stones and bark, and somehow managed to find space next to me. He set himself up comfortably, and began to beat the bark into fibre. I sang along with the elders as we worked, daydreaming about my new sibling. I wondered what my parents would name him or her, what kind of person he or she would become, and anticipated the celebrations when the hut was built and the birth string was buried.

"I see you are excited to become an elder sister." Izkah broke his silence.

I smiled. "My parents have been trying to give me a sibling for years."

"What about having your own? You are old enough to choose this year." He was prying.

A'azgimai and Layla watched through the corner of their eyes, suddenly lowering the volume of their singing.

I looked at the twisted fibres between my fingers and smiled, thinking of my beloved. "I am."

"Have you given any thought to whom you might choose?"

I knew that he wanted me. Handsome and clever though he was, my heart could not be his, it belonged to his brother. As childish as Imsaid could be at times, his heart was always sincere. I had long noticed the awkward glances and the half-moon smiles. Other men had their eyes on me, some of the married men wanted me for a second wife, and many of the bachelors looked on me, but their gaze was hungry. Izkah's gaze was hungry. Imsaid's was reverent.

I nudged him with my shoulder. "You know I am not supposed to tell you that, it would curse the union. If I make a choice, I want the gods to sow great favour upon it. I want to be with a man that loves and cherishes me. I want the right man to put his fire in my water."

"There are many hoping to make you their wife." He replied.

"I am sure that there are many women that would want to be with you Izkah." I changed the subject. "You are by far one of the most intelligent men in the village. Look at all the things you think up. Any woman would be lucky to have you."

His mouth spread into a crooked grin. "Any man would be lucky to have you."

A'azgimai and Layla snickered at me. I shot them a look. Layla went back to braiding, but A'azgimai stuck out her tongue, and then returned to work.

In the distance I saw Imsaid carrying a pair of large stones on his shoulders, clay from the pit caked into the crevices of the muscles in his back.

"And here we are two lucky charms." I mumbled. I took up another bundle of loose fibre. "Has your brother given any indication at who he might want to choose him?"

"I never asked him. He didn't seem too concerned with the ceremony" he lowered his voice so that only I could hear "though I think that A'azgimai might have an eye for him, and you know her, she always gets what she wants."

"She does." I nodded. "My cousin has a very strong will. My father says that she is more Sunshadeen than Sunshaia."

"You would know what she wants better than I, perhaps you should ask her." He suggested, as if I hadn't thought to ask her already.

"Maybe it is you she has an eye for. You and Imsaid do look alike." I said.

"But I am the handsome one." He replied. "You said so yourself."

I laughed awkwardly as I coiled the finished length of rope and added it to the pile of wound and bound rope. We braided and sang through the day. It was hard to imagine the amount of rope that went into making a new hut when looking at the finished product, but it took hours of work, and a special weave of the bark fibre to make it strong enough to support the frame. Izkah continued to pound the bark into fibres, stealing looks at me, while A'azgimai stole looks at us. Had I known that my cousin had an eye for him, I would have pressed him harder to cast his eye upon her.

"Enough, enough!" Elder Rahi clapped his hands. "Sun is about to paint the sky, it is time to pay homage and prepare our dinner! I have been smoking fish all day and I am sure you are all very hungry."

Elder Rahi had the softest heart of any in the village. He and my grandfather were cousins and they loved each other well. He may not have been as knowledgeable as elder Jahi or as spiritually inclined as my grandfather, but he was always the one I ran to when I needed guidance. His voice was calming as the tide. Whenever I would bring my concerns to him, he listened to me intently, and then asked me what the peace would demand. The answer never failed to put my mind at ease.

"Come on Izkah, let us go and help prepare the meal." I tugged at his arm. "Unless your leg is too sore to carry a basket of fish."

On our way to the smoking hut, Izkah stopped to speak to his father for a moment. I left him there and continued on with A'azgimai and Layla.

"Someone seemed very interested in your choice at the ceremony." Layla tittered. "I wonder if he is not trying to tell you something."

"He told me that A'azgimai has her eye on a special someone." I responded, deflecting the attention away from myself.

"You should be wary of assertions made by people who ask too many questions, it means they don't know anything." A'azgimai retorted as she balanced a basket of fish on her head. "Can we go and eat now?"

As the great fire was lit and the fish were given to the elders to heat over it, Sun began to paint the sky. Elder Rahi had promised us that he would sing the Song of Creation to bless the meal. The only sound sweeter than his voice when he spoke was his voice when he sang. The gods had given him a true gift.

As everyone took their seats, I noticed that Imsaid was not among us. I sat next to Izkah in the hopes that I would see him when he came to eat. Elder Rahi began to sing, but there was no Imsaid.

"I should go and get Imsaid." Izkah said. "It is almost time to eat."

He took to his feet to go and find him. This was my chance go get Imsaid alone. If what Izkah said was true about A'azgimai, I had to make my feelings for Imsaid known before the Choosing Ceremony, superstition be damned. A'azgimai gets what A'azgimai wants, but not if I get to it first.

I stood up and put my hand on Izkah's shoulder. "Do not trouble yourself. Your thigh is still sore. I will go and collect him. Just wait here and save us some leaves."

I took a breath and walked away from the village centre, following my fading shadow into ebbing light as Sun painted the sky, ending another day. Imsaid was likely washing the earth from his skin before coming to eat. When I saw him pass, his skin was caked red with clay. It was improper to sit down to a meal when one's skin is not clean, and besides, he loved the sea.

He would be alone; nude in the water, and not a pair of eyes would see him. That is until I came to see him. When I thought that no one could see I stole looks at his body, lean and muscular, made strong by long hours in the endless waters diving and catching fish. Warmth rose between my thighs. I wanted him. I had wanted him since I had flowered and he had grown into a man, but despite my friendliness, skill in the more amorous of interactions always eluded me. Sometimes I envied Layla, whether she fancied one man or another, she would have no fear in taking him into her arms. It was no crime to give in to our passions before marriage.

For some of us, that is the only way to tell if the fire that drew them together burned in their hearts or their loins. I never could, though I wanted to. I was too afraid. I would see him looking at me. I could only hope that his look meant what I hoped it did, though I was still too shy to ask. Other men looked on me, but their gaze was tainted with obvious lust. Their eyes followed me like starving cheetahs would eye a prancing deer. I ignored them. Imsaid's gaze was different.

He saw me, not just a woman he wanted. I wished that I could tell him. I could not even tell Imsaid that he was handsome to his face. I could only jest and compliment him through his brother, which I fear he took for interest. Izkah was not the one I wanted, Imsaid was. If Izkah was right, then A'azgimai wanted Imsaid for herself as well, and A'azgimai gets what A'azgimai wants.

Perhaps the Choosing Ceremony would change that. Perhaps I would bend before him and offer my water, and he would give me his fire and accept. Perhaps A'azgimai would beat me to him and stare him into relinquishing his flame. If I were to see that I would just melt. I could not let that happen.

I had reached the beach. My toes sank into the sand, still warm from the heat of the day. I scanned the water, squinting in the dying light. There I spied him, leaning back in the water, his chest rising above the surface and sinking again. As I moved in closer, I saw the water shifting around him. I smiled, though I would rather deny it, part of me knew what he was doing and was glad to catch him in the act. I watched him in silence from the edge of the water, the warm tide lapping against my toes as I bit my lip and listened to him gasp. I imagined him thinking of me, because I thought of him when I gave into my own desires.

"Imsaid." My nature found the voice that my head could not.

He fell out of his self-induced trance like a tumbling boulder. He whipped his head about in search of the voice that called him. I stifled the urge to laugh at his embarrassment and spoke again.

"Imsaid, supper will be ready soon, and Elder Rahmi is singing the Song of Creation."

"By and by I will come. I would not want to miss that. Elder Rahmi has the truest voice I have ever heard." He stayed motionless in the water, afraid to let me see his nature.

I pressed him "Then come! Unless you want to spend the whole night in the water."

"Go ahead, I will follow you." He would not cooperate. I needed to take more aggressive measures.

I waded into the water. When I reached him, I was waist deep. I took him by the arm and tugged. "Come."

He finally stood up, his wet skin of ebon glistening in the twilight. My eyes drank in his perfect form as the droplets of water ran like tiny rivers between the crevices of his musculature. His tried to hide his nature, but he was unsuccessful. I gazed at his nakedness, still fat from his self-induced gratification. I felt my skin flush with desire. I looked him in the eye and made a decision.

"Imsaid, I need to tell you something."

"What is it?"

It was too late to turn back; I looked at the water and continued to speak. "I know who I am going to choose at the ceremony."

He looked confused. "You aren't supposed to tell. The women never say who they will choose until it is time."

"I think that it is important that you know." I looked him in the eyes, he gave me that look again, full of the longing I had suspected.

It was real, and so were the feelings that permeated my every fibre. "I choose you."

He stared with his mouth open, wordless. I was beginning to regret my confession. "Are you not going to say anything, Imsaid? Are you even going to ask me why?"

"I-I, there are smarter men, there are stronger men." He replied. "Dawish is a mountain, my brother is…"

I put my finger over his mouth. "I want you because you don't think you are good enough. You will love me; I will be more than just a wife to you. I will be your life."

I kissed him. I pulled him close and I kissed him deeply. I needed to feel his skin against mine. I needed to feel his heart beat in my chest. I needed to feel his fire inside of me. I swathed him in my desire, and we sang ourselves to paradise with the music of our sighs in the rhythm of our rocking bodies. There, in the bosom of the goddess's endless waters we were unified. I could have stayed there in his arms until Sun chased away the moon and painted the colours of the dawn, but we were awaited and could not stay. As he thrust his last, grimacing in his joyful explosion of the flesh, I whispered in his ear. "I love you."

After we had committed the deed of love, we quietly made our way back to the village, where Elder Rahi was still singing. His voice flowed like honey from between his lips as he told the tale of how the gods created the world and brought life to it.

Imsaid and I chose not to sit together, looking at one another through the flames as we ate our meal. Perhaps the distance was too conspicuous. Izkah looked on us with a suspicious eye, but decided not to question us, and instead focused on his meal.

Several days had passed since our first night, and each night after we found ourselves in each other's arms, delighting in paradise of our combined forms. It was the day before the Choosing Ceremony, and the people had managed to complete construction of the hut for my mother. I had the honour of leading her to it.

"Can I look yet?"

"No, mother, keep your hand over your eyes." I said while I guided her by her free wrist.

As is our custom, when a hut is being finished for a new mother, we always sent her away until it was completed. My mother had been waiting anxiously on the other side of the village. There she sat in anticipation as we thatched the roof, smoked the walls to harden the clay, and had the elders bless it for the birth of the unborn. My father was so proud, and was beside himself with happiness when he sent me to collect her.

"Just a few more steps, mother. We are almost there." I looked over my shoulder, and saw her ivory smile, wide as the joyful moon.

When we arrived at the site behind their hut, I guided her by the waist to stand before the people, who were gathered with many gifts of fruit, hides, honey, and carvings of stone, wood and ivory. They came with grass mats and tinder for fires. They came with joyful hearts and tongues to sing.

"Open your eyes, love." My father stood before her with arms wide open.

She uncovered her eyes, and after blinking for a moment to adjust to the light, she gasped at the sea of joyful faces gathered to celebrate the life she carried and the home they had just built. She fell into my father's arms and wept in her happiness. An ululation went up from one of the elder women and the singing and clapping began.

Gift of goddess, gift to the earth,
Come forth and break water, we welcome your birth!
Welcome your birth, we welcome your birth!
Gift of the goddess, gift to the earth,
Come forth and break water, we welcome your birth!

I ululated with the other women as they showered my mother with their many gifts and formed a circle. We sang, clapped, and danced. I loved music, I loved to sing. I loved to sing with the people. Our voices melted into each other as the men joined the chorus. We circled, we sang, we clapped and we danced.

"Izkah! Come and sing with us!" Imsaid called to his brother, who only sat on the side, tapping his toe to the rhythm and not participating in the dance. It appeared that something was weighing heavy on his mind. Izkah did not accept his brother's invitation to dance. He waved Imsaid off and walked away.

Izkah was always in his own head. It was best sometimes to let him stay there. I refused to let his melancholy taint the celebration of my unborn brother or sister's birth hut. Instead, I focused on celebrating in the arms of my future husband. Our moment in the sea was forgotten by neither my mind, nor my flesh. As the people crowded in and separated into a circle, I found my way to Imsaid. I took him by the wrist and we stole away to make love again.

The desire of our flesh now quiet, we lay together in the grass, gazing into each other's eyes. The Choosing Ceremony was tomorrow, and tomorrow I would declare myself for him, and he would respond in kind. He was for me. I was for him. We were for each other.

I kissed him. "Tomorrow."

"Tomorrow."

We stealthily returned to the celebrations. The people were so wrapped in the current of their song that no one noticed that we were missing. The singing went late into the night until elder Rahmi called the proceedings to close, for tomorrow, we would celebrate again.

I barely slept that night, my mind was restless. I lay on my back, alone in my hut staring into the darkness above me, thinking about the morrow. In the morning I would paint my skin with swirls of white in homage to Sunshaia and don my finest grass skirt. Tomorrow I would dance, and sing and clap; tomorrow I would offer Imsaid my water. Tomorrow he would give me his fire. Images of the dance swirled in my mind. I imagined the sound of the people's voices, the dust thrown into the air as we danced, and the great woven cloaks worn by the men waving as they danced vigorously before us, begging to be chosen.

I was unsure of when sleep took me, it seemed like a blink. I was roused in the early morn by the call of my grandfather's great ram's horn. It was time to begin. There was a rap on my door.

"Yahuia! Yahuia! Open up!"

I wiped the sleep from my eyes and lifted the door out of the doorway. The light burst into my hut and nearly blinded me. "Good morning Layla, I thought you would be getting ready."

She let herself in. "I have been ready since last night, what happened to you? You are usually up before Sun peeks over the endless waters."

She looked exquisite. Her skin had been well oiled, and the white swirls of paint that covered her from face to foot top were perfect. The grass skirt she had been working on for weeks was colourful, and danced around her waist like trees in a gentle breeze.

"I slept late. You look good."

"Thank you. Late?" She smiled at me. "What is his name?"

"His name is mind your business." I nudged her shoulder playfully. "Since you are here you can help me comb my hair and paint my back."

"Funny you should mention that. That was why I came to you." She turned around to expose her bare brown back.

"So you painted yourself last night and neglected your back, when you could have done it fresh this morning?" I shook my head.

Layla cocked her head to the side. "No, I painted my body and left the back so that I could sleep, and now you can help me."

I shook my head and removed one of my gourds from the wall. "Where is A'azgimai?"

"Already in the village centre." Layla stood in the light and moved her thick curls away from her shoulders.

"You lie!" I began to paint her back.

"You can feed me to a hyena if I lie." Layla replied. "It seems she is eager to make her choice."

"I wonder who it could be."

"If I knew the answer to that, I would be hiding for my life. If she is choosing today, then she guarded even the notion that she would make a choice with her life."

"Perhaps she did not want to curse the union." I replied, drawing the last swirl at the small of her back and pointing to the wall. "There, finished. Now go get that hair pick and oil." I sat on the floor in the beam of light that shone through the door before Layla quickly oiled my hair and picked through it.

"You have a lot of grass in here. Yahuia you need to be more careful."

I remembered how the grass found its way into my tresses and unsuccessfully stifled a chuckle.

"Yahuia…how did you get this grass in your hair? You are keeping something from me."

"Just hurry up so that we can paint my skin and get my skirt on. I am sure it won't be long before the elders look in on us."

She pulled the pick through a knot, it stung. "Tell me."

"I would not want to taint the union and reveal the secret before I make my choice." I grimaced. "Now comb faster."

Layla rushed through with her task and arranged my tresses, our hair had to be picked and spread out as far as we could. The larger our afros, the more beautiful we looked. We then hastily painted the swirls of white to represent the water goddess before I donned my grass skirt. It was not as colourful as Layla's, then again, I did not spend countless days painting each blade of dried grass that my mother and I wove into it. Imsaid would not mind, he likely wouldn't even notice.

Elder Rahmi sounded his horn again.

"We had best get moving." Layla patted me on the shoulder. "No one is going to choose for us."

We made our way to the village centre, where the singing had already begun. The men had not yet arrived and the elders were growing impatient.

"Yahuia!" My mother called to me.

I ran to her with my arms open and embraced her.

"Watch yourself now." She pushed me back gently. "I don't want to ruin your paint. You look beautiful."

"Mother you should be resting. Why are you up so early? The choosing won't be for a while now."

She kissed my cheeks between the swirls of paint. "I would not miss this for the world. My mother was there for me when I chose, and I will be there for you. Besides, how can I complain about your choice if I am not there when you make it?"

We laughed and kissed each other's cheeks one last time before Layla grabbed me by the wrist and pulled me to the line of eligible women. I waved at her parents as we took our places.

When the eligible bachelors came, decked in their fine cloaks with skin patterned in ochre, we ululated to welcome them and began to sing. My heart was racing, the ceremony had finally begun. Elder Rahmi blew his horn, and hands clapped the rhythm while we all sang. We sang to the glory of the gods and the memory of our ancestors. We sang to the promise of love and happiness. We sang for the joy of the gift of the present and the potential of the future. I lost myself in the music; my head swam in the divine, melodious river that was our voices.

The men danced first, each of them taking a turn to perform before us, demonstrating their vitality and wordlessly making their case for being chosen. Imsaid danced first, and though my love was not a sure-footed dancer, he brought a smile to my face nonetheless. He whipped his cloak around and stomped his feet, the dust clouded around him as he did his best not to look awkward in front of me. He was fortunate that my love was not predicated on his aptitude for dancing.

Dawish took his turn, and spent his entire set with his eyes fixed on Layla. He flexed muscles and for some reason that only the gods could understand, he stood on one foot and hopped. Layla did not seem to mind, though from the perplexed and bemused looks on many of the other women's faces, she would not see much competition for his hand in marriage.

When Izkah began to dance, his movements explained his reason for being so distant. He danced, but he danced for me, ignoring the other women in the line. I looked around to avoid eye contact, and on turning my head to the side I saw a disappointed look spread across A'azgimai's face. She wanted Izkah, and he was completely ignoring her. I tried to avoid looking directly at him or A'azgimai until his dance was over. We allowed the rest of the bachelors to take their turn, and then it was our time to dance.

Each of us took our turns dancing in the space between the lines of men and women. Though we women chose, the dance allowed us to show the people the highlights of our womanhood. We swayed our hips and tossed our hair. We batted our eyes at the young men, and teased at who we might choose. When my turn came to dance,

I gave myself over to the rhythm, swaying, stomping, clapping and spinning.

The rattles on my legs shook in time to the music. The world disappeared and there was only me. I felt like I was flying. I writhed and stomped and jumped, singing while I danced. I love music. I made eye contact with Imsaid when my turn had finished, then I gave way to the others.

A'azgimai's dance was fast and angry. Seeing Izkah ignore her in such a fashion must have lit something in her. Her dance was not flirtation. My cousin was beautiful and more beautiful still when she danced, though now she showed more power than grace. She danced for none but herself. She ended her turn and the dance by kicking back the dust towards the men, an indication that she had lost interest in choosing.

After all of us had presented ourselves in the sight of the gods and the people, the elders came forth with fire and water. The bachelors were given small flaming bundles of grass, and we were given bowls full of water. The pace of the singing slowed, and the bachelors sang to us, begging to be chosen:

> *Beloved I beg you choose me! Dance I will dance!*
> *Offer your water to me! Dance I will dance!*
>
> *I'll kick up the dust for you! Dance I will dance!*
> *Tell me what I must do! Dance I will dance!*
>
> *Hear the elders singing! Dance I will dance!*
> *This is only the beginning! Dance I will dance!*
>
> *Say you'll me my wife! Dance I will dance!*
> *Together we will make a life! Dance I will dance…*

We swayed side to side, holding the water above our heads and shuffling our places in the line to add to the suspense. The men continued to sing, holding the fire above their heads and waiting for us to decide. Imsaid watched me with longing eye; I took my time dancing to him. After all, we had the rest of our lives to sing and dance together. Izkah also watched me, sadness brewing in his eyes with every step that I took towards his brother. The decision was not his to make, it was mine, and I loved Imsaid. I knelt before my beloved, offered him my water and bowed my head. I heard his fire hiss as he snuffed it in the bowl. It was sealed, we were to be married.

I raised my head, and stood up to match my eyes with his. I drank in the warmth of his gaze. I looked to see what had become of A'azgimai and Izkah, perhaps she offered him her water despite his obvious display. For a moment, I forgot who my cousin was. As I turned to look at her, I witnessed A'azgimai pouring the last of her water at her feet, and giving Izkah a look that would melt stone. Izkah did not say another word. He simply walked away. Imsaid called to him, but his efforts were in vain. Izkah would not come. He needed time to be alone.

We sang and danced late into the night, even as we prepared a feast of fish and sweet fruits, crabs and roasted plantains. To my chagrin there were no pomegranates, they were my favourite. As we sat by the fire, our bellies full and our hearts warm, I sensed that Imsaid was unsettled.

"I should go and look for him, he must be so embarrassed."

"Stay with me beloved," I held him tighter. "Give him time, he will come back. He has to stand for you at the wedding does he not?"

He smelled like the sea.

Imsaid's lips curled into a smile. "He does."

As the night wore on, the elders took it upon themselves, as they did at every Choosing Ceremony, to share with us the wisdom of their years. Some would say listen, other would say be strong. Some would say take time for self; others would repeat the message that we are stronger together. The only constant advice was that that the success of our unions was the foundation of our peace. The gods smiled on us, and though Sun had given way to the night, I felt the warmth of their affection. I felt blessed.

In the days following the Choosing Ceremony, the whole village was at work again building new huts. Though we had chosen our future husbands, our weddings would have to wait until our marital homes were built. I divided my time between braiding rope for the new huts and preparing the interior of the birth hut for my mother.

My days were long, and I was always tired at the end of them, but the joy I felt was worth the fatigue. Every morning Imsaid and I would share food together in front of the hut he shared with Izkah. At first I worried about the awkwardness of seeing him there, but it had been several days and he had not returned. Now I worried about where he had gone, and when he would return.

This was not the first time Izkah had gone on a long walk. There were times when he would feel particularly restless, and that would drive him to disappear into the wilderness. He would always return with something interesting, like the tusks of a dead elephant he found, or a handful of precious stones. In those times, he would at least tell someone where he went. He had not been seen since the Choosing Ceremony. I hid my anxiety from Imsaid. It took much for me to convince him to forego searching for his brother. They shared a divine fire, and though they were so different, Imsaid was restless without his brother. A kiss, kind word, and quick joining would serve to calm his storm. Imsaid would return for there was no other place to go. This was home.

I was hard at work in the new birth hut, laying out grass mats, freshly tanned hides, and securing the straps to hold my mother's legs apart when the child broke water. I sat for a moment, looking at this place the people built together. So long as we were together, there was nothing that we could not accomplish. Truly, our unity was a thing of beauty. Life would soon be made here, and I was eager to help my mother usher it into the world.

"Yahuia." A voice called from outside the hut.

"Yes."

"May I come in?" It was Izkah.

I shot to my feet and pushed the hide away from the doorway. "Izkah! Where did you go? No one has seen or heard from you since the ceremony."

He looked at his feet. "I-I needed to go for a walk. I brought you something."

He took his hands from behind his back produced my favourite fruit.

"A pomegranate! Where did you get this?"

"From a tree."

I clicked my tongue and tried to swipe it from his hand. He was too fast for me.

"Let me cut it for you."

I stepped backwards into the hut. "Come in, I am just about finished preparing the hut. I am excited to show you what I have done." When he entered, I proudly showed him all of the preparations I had made for the upcoming birth. "I finally finished preparing the straps for binding her feet and dug the pit for the birth string to be buried. I am waiting for my father to finish preparing the hides for the floor and I still need to weave a basket for him, or her, to sleep. I am sure that it is going to be a girl."

Izkah listened with interest, watching me as I fluttered around showing off what I had done.

"Here, take your fruit." He held the cut peace, offering to me.

"Do you not want any?"

He smiled at me in that way he does. "I have had plenty. If I eat any more I might swell up and turn red."

I took a bite. It was tart and slightly cool. My eyes rolled back into my head as I munched away, filling my mouth with the juice. It was the most delicious pomegranate I had ever tasted.

"Yahuia, I need to tell you something."

"What?" My head started to feel light, and my vison began to blur. Either I was eating too fast, or there was something wrong with the fruit.

"It's about your marriage to Imsaid."

I fell into darkness; I felt my consciousness floating between dreaming and the waking world. I saw Imsaid. He kissed me. He embraced me. I reciprocated. "Where is Izkah?" I asked him between kisses.

He pulled back to answer me, but fell again into my kisses, and we fell into each other's arms. Something felt different about the way he touched me, the way he moved inside of me. The headiness subsided, and I opened my eyes to look upon him. The blurred face above me and manhood inside of me were not my Imsaid, he did not smell like the sea.

"Izkah, what are you doing?"

He gripped me tighter and I felt him deeper inside of me. "Loving you, Yahuia. Tell me again that you want to marry me."

"No." The horror of what was happening to me jolted me back into my right mind. I thrashed my hips and pushed him away, I wanted him off of me, out of me. "Izkah stop!"

"But you love me." He was strong and pressed me harder, it hurt me. "You said that you loved me."

"No!" I cut his shoulder with my nails and shouted in his face. "Get off me!"

He pulled away from me, looking at me as if I had broken a promise I never made. Something was wrong with his eyes; they were black and dead-looking. My rage would not allow me to question my discovery any further.

I grabbed a roll of rope and whipped him with it while he covered his head and backed away. "GET OUT! GET OUT! GET OUUUUUUT!"

I managed to put a few more welts in his back as he scampered from the hut and out of my sight. I stood there, my trembling hands squeezing the chord and my chest heaving. He violated me. He tricked me and violated me with some fell illusion. When the sound of his footfalls had faded into the distance, I dropped the rope and fell to my knees. I wept. I wept and bowed my head in prayer to the goddess, begging her to have mercy and make me forget what had just happened.

I have not the slightest idea how long I stayed there, my eyes overflowing with manifestations of my pain and rage. I could not put my feelings into words. I could only wonder what Imsaid would do if he found out. He must never find out. I must keep the peace, even though Izkah had broken it. Love was given freely among the people, but only when the women were willing. No man had ever crossed this threshold. Only the gods knew what would happen. In that moment, all I could do was weep and rock.

"Yahuia, Yahuia?" It was my beloved calling. I could not bear to see him and so I did my utmost to remain silent.

My failed attempts to stifle my sobbing rendered the enterprise fruitless, and he found me.

"Yahuia!"

I raised my eyes to look upon his countenance, so much like his brother and yet so different. Tears came again and overflowed like a river during a monsoon.

He ran up to me and tried to comfort me with affectations. I held him at bay with an outstretched arm. I did not want to be touched. "No! No!"

"What happened? Please! Tell me!" He knelt before me. "Have I done something?"

I could not speak, nor look on him again, his eyes were wide with concern. I shook my head.

"Has someone hurt you?"

The words caught in my throat.

"Yahuia! Who has hurt you? Tell me so that I can bring it to the elders. Tell me what happened!" Imsaid implored.

"Ask your brother."

"What did Izkah do to you?" The anxiety in him could not be hidden by even the best of liars.

"I can't." I sobbed and shook my head. "I can't."

He took my hand and kissed it. "I swear to you Yahuia, whatever has happened, whatever it is, I promise that you will be blameless. Tell me what happened."

I could not answer.

He placed a gentle hand on my chin and bid me look on him. "Look at me. Look at me. You are safe here with me. Tell me what has happened so that I may set it right."

"Do you swear to the gods and on the heads of our ancestors that you will keep the peace, no matter what I tell you?"

He kissed his fingers and touched the seat of his divine fire.

"Last night I was here preparing the hut for my mother and Izkah came to see me." I sniffled. "He returned from his long walk and it seemed that he was here to make amends. He offered me a pomegranate as a peace offering. He cut it open and gave me a wedge. When I ate it, something happened, and when I came to my senses..." I could not bear to speak the words, I trembled.

"Hush, hush." He pulled me to his chest. He smelled like the sea. "What happened?"

I swelled my chest with air, counted my heartbeats, and then I told him.

"He was on top of me, inside of me. I told him to get off, but he told me that I swore to love him, that I would marry him, that I wanted him. I never said such things. I never wanted him. I couldn't stop him. I scratched him and I shouted. I lashed at him with the cord and told him to leave. His eyes…his eyes were not the same. He ran into the night and left me here."

I heard his heart race in his chest, and I cried. My tears wet his chest. He kissed my forehead tenderly. He smelled of the sea, and now the calm and playful sea had been overtaken by a storm.

"I need you to come with me," He said as sweetly as his anger would allow. "Izkah cannot be allowed to do this to you and go unpunished."

"No." I shook my head. "No."

I was terrified.

He took my hand and took to his feet, doing his best to reassure me. "I will keep you safe. No angry hand shall touch you so long as I am with you. Come and let us find you justice."

I wrapped my arms around him and held him close. I did not want to leave the hut. I felt safe here, safe with him, and safe from his brother. Imsaid would not have it. He took me by the wrist and pulled me behind him to the village to confront his brother. No good would come of this.

"Izkah!" He bellowed, his grip tightening on my wrist. "IZKAH! IZKAAAAAH!"

"Imsaid, what is wrong with you?" His father came to maintain the peace. "What vexes you so my son, why do you shout?"

My mother and that of Imsaid overheard the commotion and came see about it. "What is wrong with Yahuia?" Imsaid's mother asked.

"Ask my brother." He would not let me speak. Rage had taken over. "IZKAAAAAAAH!"

The people came, many of them begging for Imsaid to calm himself and explain his ire. He had no time for this. He took off like a voracious cheetah into the crowd in pursuit of his brother, who attempted to slink away from the disturbance.

I tried to run after him, but my feet would not carry me. My knees buckled and I fell into my mother's arms.

"Youbayouni! Help me!" she shouted to Imsaid's mother.

They each took an arm and tried to sit me down. I would not. I shook myself from their grip, vision blurred from tears and anger. I ran behind the crowd and forced myself through the bustling throng, following Imsaid's shouts.

"WHY? WHY? Tell them what you did to Yahuia!"

A wave of gasps washed over the people. As I finally pushed through them, I saw Imsaid on his back, blood leaking from a stab wound to his belly. Izkah was on his back as well, wrestled to the ground by Dawish, A'azgimai and a few others.

"NOOOOOOO!" I fell to my knees at his side, trying to lift his head as he slowly went limp. I cradled him at my bosom, and implored Sunshaia to beg clemency from Sunshadeen and let my beloved live. I begged with all the love that lived in me. I offered them all that I had, and yet my orations could not dissuade Sunshadeen from claiming his due. Imsaid breathed his last and the fire god took from him the divine fire loaned to him at birth. I begged him not to die, but by the time I found the words, he was already gone.

There were no words to give meaning to the depth of my agony. All I had were my screams. I screamed. I screamed his name. I screamed for the gods. I screamed my anguish for all the people to hear. I screamed until my mother and father pulled me away from my beloved's corpse and the crowd. I was too weak to resist. I turned my head to see Youbayouni and Tarig kneeling over their son's body, struck dumb by the horror and grief of watching one of their sons murder the other.

My parents took me to their hut and lay me down on their own sleeping furs. Though my legs were weak, and my arms trembled, somehow I found strength enough to scream. The image of Imsaid laid low and bloodied flashed in my mind each time I closed my eyes. Their efforts to calm me were fruitless. The only thing that quieted my hysteria was the fatigue of screaming out my anguish. Sleep took me, for how long, only the gods knew.

I awoke to Elder Rahmi, my grandfather, caressing my cheek and mumbling words of comfort I was too drowsy to hear. I opened my eyes and looked on his aged face. Though his expression was stoic, his eyes spoke volumes about his fears for me.

"Yahuia, my granddaughter." Elder Rahmi cooed "Did you sleep well?"

It took me a moment to rub the sleep from my eyes, and for the full horror of witnessing my beloved's death to settle into my mind. I could not answer him. I only shook my head, for now that my Imsaid was gone, nothing could be well for me.

"Can you speak to me, my Yahuia?" He asked, his rough hand on my cheek.

I kissed his palm and looked up at him. "Yes, Elder Rahmi."

He smiled as warmly as I had ever seen him. "We are not in company, you may call me grandfather."

I relaxed a little "Yes, grandfather."

"I need to ask you some difficult questions. Can you answer them for me?"

I knew what he was going to ask me, and as much as it pained me to relive the details of Izkah's crime against my flesh, if Imsaid were to ever receive justice, if I were to ever receive justice, I would have to tell him.

"You want to know why Imsaid and Izkah broke the peace."

"Yes my child. Tell me why they were arguing. Imsaid mentioned that Izkah had done something to you. Did he hurt you?"

I nodded.

"I see no bruises or broken bones, what did he do?" Even my elder, as wise as he was, seemed to have a hard time understanding what had transpired.

"You and the elders will pass judgement on him soon won't you?" I asked.

He nodded and gestured for me to speak.

There was no word for what he had done; the thought of it had never entered the minds of the people. "He forced himself on me."

"What do you mean?" His voice was gentler than usual. He did not want to upset me further.

I explained in detail what Izkah had done. It took a frustrating amount of convincing for my grandfather to understand that I gave no consent to Izkah. I told him of how enraged Imsaid had become when I told him what Izkah had done. There was no stopping Imsaid. He wanted justice for me, though neither he nor I knew what justice looked like for Izkah's crime against me. Stolen tools, food, or hides can be recompensed with equal value. How does one repay stolen love or life? Love can be returned with love, but only when freely given. Life can be shared and given. However, once taken it cannot be returned to the fallen in equal measure. If only the gods would speak to us and tell us what was right to do. I saw in the eyes of my elder that even he in his time-earned wisdom was lost.

He gently took my wrist into his hand "I need you to come with me. The people are gathering and they expect an answer from the elders."

I pulled my wrist back "I do not want to go."

My heart was racing at the thought of having to see their faces again. I was sure that some of them blamed me. Perhaps they thought was playing with the two of them and caused rancour between them. I could not see their faces. I still felt unclean. I know that it was not my fault, but I felt the fool for trusting Izkah. I would never trust another man again. I could not bear to look on him either. I was so full of anger that I may have visited upon him the very crime he committed against my beloved. It was better that I not see him. I still felt weak, and I needed more rest.

My grandfather respected my wishes and carried my testimonial to the other elders, leaving me to rest and wonder what would become of Izkah. Imsaid had not even been put on a pyre yet. I wanted to be there when his parents gave him to Sunshadeen in the sacred flames, despite the looks and comments that I feared. I lay my head back and drowned in the flood of thoughts that surged through my head, sinking into back into slumber with the hopes of forgetting.

I dreamt that night. I was walking by the sea. It was calm and blue, the waves gently caressing the beach. It was peaceful. However, the tranquillity would not last. I heard a woman sobbing. She sat naked on the beach, her long black curls wrapped over her body like a cloak. I had never seen her before, and yet I felt that I knew her. I went to comfort her, offering my embrace. She hung her head and fell into my arms. She smelled like the sea. I did not see her face, but I felt her tears wetting my skin. I asked her why she cried. She only answered with more tears, and a tighter embrace. I held her close and rested my chin on the crown of her head.

I asked her again. "Wherefore do you cry?"

"I cry for you." She replied. "I cry for you."

"What do you mean?" The tide grew, beating against the shoreline more aggressively with each succession of waves.

"I cry for you." She repeated. "I cry for you, I love you, my child, and I feel all of your pain."

The sea level was rising, the now red waters splashed up against our legs.

"Come. We should go, the water is rising."

She did not speak, she only held me close and would not release me when I tried to stand.

"Come, we need to go, the water is rising, we need to go now!"

I struggled, but her grip was too strong. The water had now risen to our shoulders, and still she would not release me.

She turned her face towards me, and to my horror, I saw nothing. There was blank flesh where her face should have been. No eyes, no nose, no mouth. I panicked and tried again to escape her stone grip, the water was now under my chin.

"Innocence has ended." She said before disappearing under the crimson waters, which soon overtook me as well.

I jolted awake and sat up on my sleeping furs, my skin soaked with sweat and my chest pounding with anxiety.

"NO!" I heard a voice cry from outside.

I rose to my feet and ran to the doorway. I lifted the door out of the way and looked outside. At first I saw nothing, but I heard the commotion. I tied my loincloth and ran out the door in the direction of the shouting. The cacophony of angry voices grew louder as I approached the village centre. I could not make out what anyone was saying, there was shoving and shouting. Some people were crying, while others were waving their fists in rage. Some of the men even struck one another.

"You know who killed him! Admit it!" shouted one of the men. "It had to be your family that did it!"

The man he was shouting at responded with a shove to the chest. "What kind of person do you take me for? If I knew ho had done it I would have given him all sweet fruits I could carry. He should have been killed for what he did!"

In my heart of hearts I knew of whom they were speaking, but my curiosity could not help but seek to confirm my intuition.

"Who are you talking about? Who was killed?"

They looked on me and hung their heads.

"Who is dead?" I stepped towards them. "Who has died, who was killed?"

They still would not answer.

"It was Izkah." Layla's tearful voice echoed in my ears. "Someone murdered him in the night, choked the life out of him."

Of all the things that I could have said, I found myself wanting for words. My lip quivered and my knees buckled. Izkah was dead; someone murdered him in the night. As furious as I was with him for the harm he had done, violating me, murdering his brother, my beloved, I did not wish him dead. That was not our way. As I looked upon the sea of angry faces, pointing fingers, and shoving arms, I realized that our way was broken. The people were no longer one.

I felt Layla's arms wrap around me and pull me to my feet. "Come, Yahuia, we will seek out your grandfather and your parents."

I did not speak or resist, I let her take me by the arm and pull me around the chaos that boiled over in the heart of the village. This place, this sacred place where we once sang and danced as one, where we built each other's homes, celebrated our children and chose our husbands, was now a place overflowing with anger.

"Yahuia." My mother called to me as Layla and I approached my grandfather's hut. She took me into her arms and kissed my cheeks. Her face was wet with tears. "Thank you Layla, you should go and see to your family. Yahuia, I have something to tell you."

Layla nodded her head and left us to our privacy.

"Izkah is dead. I know. He was killed in the night. By whose hand?"

"No one knows, and so they are all blaming each other." My father sighed as he wrapped us both in his long arms.

I looked to my grandfather, sitting on his stool, cradling his head in his hands.

"Why would someone do this?" I asked as my parents' arms opened.

My father rubbed his eyes in frustration. "The elders could not agree on what was to be done with him. Elder Rahi wanted forgiveness, you grandfather wanted exile, and Elder Jahi wanted blood for blood, and no one could agree. Sunshaia was merciful to you and let you sleep through it all. The arguments were bitter, and it turned the people against each other. Those who sided with Elder Rahi were called weak by those who supported Elder Jahi, and those were accused of being no less murderous than Izkah by those who supported your grandfather. Those who supported your grandfather were accused of being even more malicious than those who supported Elder Jahi, and the cycle continued. It had gotten so bad that Dawish tried to push past the men set to keep Izkah in his hut to put an end to the debate. He was stopped by Izkah's mother, but the arguments continued throughout the day yesterday. Now this morning when his mother brought food to him, she found him dead, his neck broken and his throat crushed."

I covered my mouth in horror. "Who could have been strong enough to have done this?"

"Fingers point to Dawish, but Elder Jahi will not have his grandson held culpable for Izkah's death." My mother hid her face in her hands. "The Sunbaka has come among the people and poisoned us."

I called to my grandfather. "Grandfather, what is to be done? Can we save the peace?"

He did not raise his head from his hands. "The peace is dead, my Yahuia, the peace is dead. The people are far too divided now. All the years since Sunshadeen first breathed divine fire into the people and I should live to bear witness to the death of our unity."

I knelt at his feet and pulled his hands away from his face. "Grandfather, can you not call the other elders, and together demand a return to the peace? Surely, they will listen to you. Please, you have to try."

My heart was hurting. I was unsure of what pained me more, Izkah's betrayal of our friendship, the death of Imsaid, or the chaos that overtook our village. Tears came, and I begged him again. I kissed his knuckles and begged by grandfather to try to rebuild the peace.

He looked at me with those loving brown eyes and placed a hand on my cheek, wiping my tear away with his thumb. "For you, my Yahuia, I will try."

He took a deep breath and heaved himself off of the stool and onto his feet. He took me by the hand and pulled me along. I followed him to the village centre, where the arguments still raged.

"O people!" He raised his hands.

The people did not hear him; they continued to fight amongst themselves. My grandfather took the ram's horn from his waist and blew it into the air. It droned angrily and drowned the shouting into silence. The arguments stopped and the people watched him with their full attention.

"Where are the other elders?" he asked.

"Here am I." Elder Rahi emerged from the crowd, his wizened face twisted into a wounded scowl.

"Here am I." Elder Jahi stood near the fire pit, his arms crossed.

"Jahi, Rahi, we must bring back the peace." Elder Rahmi returned the ram's horn to his waistband and held out his hand. "Please, all of these are our kin, and it pains me deeply to see such enmity spilling over them. Let us be the first to return the peace."

The other elders looked at each other and paused for a moment. All the eyes of the people were upon them.

Elder Rahi was the first to take my grandfather's hand. "I am for the peace. Jahi?"

Elder Jahi looked at their hands. "Will you apologize for accusing me of ordering Izkah's death?"

"I apologize." Elder Rahi replied.

"I too." Elder Rahmi nodded.

He added his hand to the other two. "Then I am also for the peace."

There was silence for a moment, then the people began to reconcile. Shaking hands and embracing, apologizing for the cruel things that they had said and done to one another. This was our way, peace was our way.

"No!" a woman's voice called out. It was Youbayouni, the twins' mother. Her hair was dishevelled, her lips were chapped, and her eyes were wild. Her husband tried to pull her back but she would to be silenced. "No! Where is the justice? You have your peace but where is mine? My sons are dead! My sons are DEAD! Imsaid was killed by Izkah, yes! But who now will recompense me the death of my lzkah? Call him what you will, condemn him if you must but he was my son! He was my last son! Who now will burn me when Sunshadeen comes for my divine fire? Who now will carry my husband's name another generation? You embrace and reconcile while my line remains broken, while my heart remains broken! Say what you will, deny it if you must but Elder Jahi you, YOU were the one to put his death in the minds of the people. Whether it was your word, your order, or your black heart, YOU are to blame for the death of my Izkah! YOU! How will you repay me? How will you recompense me? Izkah did wrong, but he was MY SON!"

"Youbayouni, we are sorry for your losses. The gods know that we are. Their deaths have wounded us all." Elder Rahi stepped forward, his arms outstretched. "They were my great grandsons, I feel your pain."

"Grandfather, you feel my pain?" Her face was beset with grief. "You feel my pain? What do you know of the pain of a child breaking water and pressing them forth from your WOMB into life? What do you know of suckling a new born babe at your breast and praying to the gods that they grow strong? What do you know of nurturing them, living your every breath for them, only to have them snatched away from you? I have to burn their bodies, they were supposed to live and do this for me!"

Jahi stepped forward with his arms open. "I am sorry, Youbayouni, I am sorry. Please, come and let us make peace, let us heal together."

She watched him in silence, her eyes full of anguish and ire.

"Youbayouni, please, come." Elder Jahi invited her in again.

She stepped forward, and in the blink of an eye, a knife appeared from her waistband and she lashed out at the elder, cutting his arm.

"I will kill you!" She shrieked, flailing at him and waving the knife.

In an instant, Dawish, followed by Elder Jahi's other grandsons surged forward and tackled her to the ground. All the while she screamed and flailed, swinging the knife this way and that, trying to draw some blood.

"Youbayouni!" Tarig came running and started to push

Elder Jahi's grandsons off of his wife. "Get off of her, get off of…"

When Dawish and the others had parted, Tarig looked down at her. "Youbayouni."

There was no answer.

"Youbayouni!" He shook her, but she was unresponsive.

"You killed her! YOU KILLED HER!"

Tarig gripped Youbayouni to his chest and rocked back and forth. "You animals! You killed her!"

"Jahi, what are you going to do about this?" Elder Rahi trembled with anger. Youbayouni was his granddaughter. "Your grandsons must leave! They murdered my granddaughter!"

"They did not murder her!" Elder Jahi retorted. "They were protecting me; your granddaughter was going to kill me! Have you no concern for that?"

I had never seen Elder Rahi so angry. "But you are alive and she is not! Here she lies low at the hand of your progeny! You and your kin seem too warm to the idea of killing. Perhaps it was your order that killed Izkah!"

The people began to rumble again, fingers were pointed between families. Fingers pointed back, and all the while Tarig wept and embraced his dead wife.

"Stop it, both of you!" Elder Rahmi shouted. "Look at what you are doing."

"You will be silent Rahmi, were it not for the freeness of your granddaughter, my great grandsons would still be alive; my granddaughter would still be alive!" Elder Rahi's tongue was not so gentle anymore; it was sharpened by his shock and grief.

"I WILL NOT have you speak of my Yahuia in this way; she was the victim of YOUR Izkah's lust." My grandfather loved me.

"Are you going to kill me or mine as well?" Elder Rahi beat his chest, tears flowing from his eyes. "It is not safe for us here. I and my progeny are leaving! The Sunbaka take you all!"

"Rahi, where will you go?" Elder Rahmi softened his tone.

"Away from here. You are all corrupt, and I cannot bear to watch your faces or the faces of your loose and murderous kin any longer!" Elder Rahi stormed off, followed by his kin.

"Jahi. Please go speak to him." Elder Rahmi wiped his palm over his face.

Elder Jahi shook his head. "Never will I look on his face again. Let him go. In fact, I am going to leave as well. This place is tainted. The gods no longer live here. Look at us, fighting one another like hyenas. Look on the blood from my arm. Rahi has some nerve to call mine murderous when it was his own Izkah that first drew blood, and in the fashion of his line, his granddaughter came to exact the same from me. I will not, I will not stay in this corrupted place. I and all those who would follow me will be gone when Sun paints the sky in the morrow, and such will be the last time you shall ever see or hear of us again." With that, he turned his back and stormed off.

Elders Rahi and Jahi made good on their promises to leave, as did their kin. When the morrow came, the people were no longer one. Elder Jahi took his family to place where Sun sets, and Elder Rahi took his south, as far away from us as the gods would allow. I watched them disappear over the horizon, swallowed by the distance and gone forever. The village was almost empty. Those that remained among us were either too loyal to my grandfather, or too afraid to go into the wide unknown. They did not sing that day, they did not sing for a long time. Grief had robbed the desire to sing from their lips, and only left them with sorrow.

Though song had gone from them for the time being, it still lived in me. My heart hurt too much to stay silent, so I sang. To the gods I sang. I sang alone. I sang of the memories of my beloved Imsaid. I loved him. His heart was kind and his eyes were playful. He was sweet, and his tongue was quick. His laughter was music to me. I loved to watch him run along the shoreline with his brother. The light of the gods made his flawless earthen skin glow like polished wood of ebon. I would fill my eyes with the sight of him kicking up sand in his wake near the endless glistening waters. O beloved! I would lay in your arms 'till Sun tires of crossing the sky, and even then I would hold you still in the darkness

Epilogue

The last of the poets bowed and left the stage to a standing ovation from the crowd, peppered with ululations. The Great Sage clapped his hands in his usual reserved fashion.

"That was rather excellent, don't you think, Captain Shahad?" Tikurkebre looked to his bodyguard.

"Amazing, O Great Sage." The captain replied.

Tikurkebre stroked his beard. "I want to see the girl."

"Which girl, O Great Sage?"

"That last one, the one that sang Yahuia's Desire. I want to see her. Bring her to me." He waved his hand towards the stage.

"You heard the Great Sage, bring her!" The captain commanded his men.

Two of them bowed before leaving the gallery. A moment later they returned with the actress. She was as beautiful as the subject of her song. Her skin was black and flawless, glowing against the flickering lamplight, free hanging braids framed her round and comely face. The Great Sage extended his hand and offered his ring. She hesitantly stepped forward and kissed it.

"All hail the Great Sage." She said with her eyes fixed on the floor.

"Look on me."

She obeyed. Her eyes shimmered in the light like polished obsidian.

"You are not from Bakar." The Great Sage's voice droned. "You are not a Jahisha. Tell me, from whence do you come?"

"Dzakira, O Great Sage." She replied. "I came with my troupe to sing for the festival."

"Will you sing again for me?" He met her eyes with his piercing gaze.

"Wha-what would you have me sing, O Great Sage?" She hung her head again, her hands visibly trembling.

Tikurkebre smiled, her fear was inviting. "Whatever you wish, for me in my private chamber at the ziggurat."

She opened her mouth to speak, but no words came.

The Great Sage snapped his fingers. "Captain, have her carried to my chamber, and find her something fine to wear. What is your name girl?"

"Gelila." She replied.

"Gelila, please me and you shall be richly rewarded." Tikurkebre rose to his feet and waved to his Barukdzin, ordering them in the Old Tongue "*Yallanu, dzutnu duaratou*[17]."

"*Naim, O Yashnusunabra*[18]." The largest of the creatures bowed before leading the others out to collect the sedan chair that bore their lord.

Tikurkebre returned to the ziggurat with his procession, Gelila in tow. In his stately chamber, Tikurkebre awaited her in his bed clad in a simple tunic and salwar. His back resting against the headboard, the Great Sage was surrounded by the silk curtains hanging from his canopy. The air was thick with the smell of myrrh and the sweet oils in his lamps. He munched on water berries, the crimson juice collecting at the corners of his mouth, waiting patiently for Gelila. Her dusky splendour had not left his mind's eye since he had heard her sing with such a transcendent voice.

There was a knock at the door.

"Enter." Tikurkebre called out.

The gilded door creaked open, and in came Gelila, swathed in the finest kaftan from the temple offerings.

"Hail, O Great Sage." She bowed. "Shall I sing for you?"

"Sing to me of far off places."

Gelila cleared her throat and began.

> *O! We the Rahisheen who know no borders,*
> *We ride like wind dervishes to the Sunya's corners,*

---

[17] Go, bring my chair
[18] Yes O Great Sage

No enemy among us shall cause us to beg for quarter,
Astride our camels and horses, long in our sandals,
We need no city walls to guard us from vandals
Our women are our treasure and honour our mantle,
Let us take what we will from Sunshaia's gifts,
Share it among our families for we shall bear no rifts,
Come together we always will to share benefits,

While she sang, Tikurkebre eyed her beauty. He watched her delicate neck as it flexed with each note, her full blackberry lips as they caressed each syllable, and her delicate hands as she accented her verses with graceful gesticulations. His passions rose, but he waited patiently for her to finish.

O beloved Rahisheen, sing together by the firelight,
Our sons are strong and our daughters a pleasing sight,
No other clans in the Sunya can understand our delight,
We the seed of merciful Elder Rahi do make love our law,
Protect our families and clans for to us this is all,
No matter what the cost we stand for the call,
So sing O Rahisheen and let us eat together,
Milk and meat are plenty and Sun gives us good weather,
Though the land be dry and harsh at times
we could never ask for better.

"Wonderful!" He clapped his hands. "Wonderful!"
Gelila bowed her head. "Thank you, O Great Sage."
"So, you are a Rahisheen are you?" Tikurkebre place the bowl on his side table and rose from his bed. "Dzakira is a long way from the Outlands. I have not seen a Rahisheen woman in some time."
He slid his long feet into a pair of sandals, and walked towards her, his sandals clapping against the veiny marble floor.
"I am glad to know that I have pleased you with my song and my presence, O Great Sage." She knelt before him.
"My dear, you have entertained me, but you have not pleased me, yet." He stood before her and wrapped his long hands around her petite shoulders. "Now that I look on you, your face is familiar."

"It should be, O Great Sage." Her voice steadied and her wide eyes closed to a squint.

"And why is that?"

Without another word, Gelila unleased a flurry of stabbing attacks on the Tikurkebre, holding him close by the collar so that he could not reach around to strike her. He stumbled backwards and lost his balance, landing on his back in the bed. Gelila straddled him with the knife held high while he gasped for air.

"My mother was a singer, and now she is a Mazkhee, you changed her with that sacred blood of yours. You did to her what you tried to do to me, and now you are dead."

With that final word, she dealt the death blow, and the Great Sage of Bakar was dead. Soon after, Gelila turned the knife on herself, robbing the Dark Sages of their justice.

THE LIONESS
OF
THE GREEN SEA

<u>Prologue</u>

I smiled at them, the two gems that gave my life light and meaning. The many sons that my wife gave to me were my pride, but she and our daughter were my heart. Tsion was beautiful, her flesh painted in the hues of the night, and her face so fine Sunshadeen must have sculpted her for the delight of my eyes. Not one other negus[19] in the Horn could dare to claim a wife, concubine, or mistress more lovely, graceful, or kind of heart than she. My daughter was brave, curious, and overflowing with wit. In truth her nature mirrored mine more than any of my seven sons or three daughters. Her smile was the delight of my heart.

I leaned in the doorway and listened to the exchange between my wife and daughter as my little Gete tried to negotiate her way out of bedtime.

"Ama, I don't want to go to sleep!" Gete squeaked in that tiny seven year old voice of hers.

"Now Gete, you know that you should be sleeping, it is too late for you to be awake." My beloved kissed her on the forehead.

"But today is a special day!" she replied, her onyx eyes wide as saucers. "All seven of my brothers are married at the same time and you are sending me to bed before the wedding feast."

"Correction, your father and I are sending you to bed before the wedding feast my dear. You are too young to be around that much drinking, my Gete, now sleep. I promise we will save some dabo[20] and honey just for you." Tsion pulled the covers up to Gete's chin.

"But I can't sleep, Ama." She continued to protest. "I would rather be dancing with you and Abbu. This is not fair."

Tsion stifled a chuckle. "Neither the fairness nor the necessity of your staying in bed tonight are up for debate tonight, my Gete."

"But look at my face! You can't say no to this face!" She scrunched her nose and smiled, two of her teeth missing in the front.

---

[19] King
[20] Bread

"Dejen, come and deal with your daughter." Tsion could disguise her amusement no longer. "Bore her to sleep with one of your stories."

I swaggered into the room, my waist-length locks swaying with my footfalls. I adjusted the gilded shawl around my shoulders and sat at the corner of my daughter's bed. "Gete."

"Yes, Abbu." She giggled.

I patted her on the leg. "What can I give you to make you go to sleep when the promise of dabo and honey are not enough?" I asked her. "Will you come and ride Asahshadeen with me tomorrow?"

"Not enough." She shook her head defiantly "One day I will have my own."

I raised my eyebrows. "Perhaps I can persuade you with another pretty kemis?"

"I have plenty. What else have you got for me?" She crossed her arms.

"Well, dabo and honey is not enough, riding my lion is not enough – AH! Perhaps there IS something that I can give you that you will sleep for." I playfully stroked the white stripe that divided my pointed beard. From the corner of my eye I could see my wife smiling and rolling eyes.

"What is it?" Gete's interest was piqued.

"Have you ever heard of Negast[21] Sebele?"

"No, who is she?" Gete sat up at full attention. "Do we know her?"

"Negast Sebele was the first of our clan to ride a lion, and the first woman to be crowned queen of Murhad." I declared with my nose in the air. "She was brave, she was strong, and she was fearless!"

"I like her already." Gete replied, giving me her full attention.

"Dejen, your story had best be quick, the guests are waiting on us, and we would not want to miss our own coffee ceremony." Tsion urged.

"Patience, my love, they will likely be too drunk to notice our absence. Besides, I am the negus and you are the negast. The main

---

[21] Queen

event can wait on us." I replied. "For now let them eat, drink, and be merry. Send a servant to tell Captain Yekob that we are delayed, but coming shortly."

"As you wish your majesty, but do not tarry too long." Tsion said in a playful tone. She stuck her head out of the door and quietly whispered my orders to the guards.

"Then I had best make this story quick!" I returned my attention to Gete. "Now, my little lioness, where do we begin the story? Ah! It begins many years ago in the Green Sea. All the clans of the Horn had been in war after war after war. I suppose that some things never change unless we make them. Negast Sebele's time was no different."

<u>Broken Pride</u>

(4,500 years before the War of Banishment)

Sebele stared blankly through her carriage window at the verdant countryside of the Horn. The rolling hills teemed with life. Beasts both great and small of every persuasion grazed, galloped, and hunted as far as the eye could see. The sky was clear, and the sweet smell of the tall grasses overpowered even the pungent odour of the striped horses ridden by the royal guard. The journey had been many weeks long from the seat of her father's power in Murhad across Burning River and the Green Sea and to the coastal city of Mah, which sat high on a hill overlooking Black Cove. It was the home of Negus Beka, chief of the Black Seal clan and ruler of the lands south of the river. Negus Yohannes had travelled to Mah in order to discuss terms of an alliance and Princess Sebele's marriage to Negus Beka's son and heir, Crown Prince Negasi.

"O Negus, we have almost arrived at Mah. Shall I send a man ahead to announce your arrival?" Captain Tedros' turbaned head bounced up and down in the window frame as his horse trotted alongside the carriage.

Negus Yohannes waved his thick umber hand. "Send a man ahead and announce us. It will give Negus Beka a chance to get the coffee going."

Negus Yohannes was a tall man with broad shoulders, made broader still by his black and gold royal cloak. His face was flat and handsome. He had high cheek bones and midnight eyes that shimmered like the opals in the golden crown nestled among his shoulder length locks. He occupied the lion's share of his side of the carriage.

"Finally! Abbu I am tired of riding in this carriage. I can barely feel my legs, and Sebele's breath is going to suffocate me."

Sebele responded with an elbow to her brother's ribs. "You are one to talk Temesgen! Your breath smells like elephant shit."

"Sebele! Watch your tongue before I wipe it with soap."

Negast Menin pointed her finger at the princess. "You are going to meet your future husband, please do not embarrass us."

Negast Menin was beautiful. Her honey brown eyes were fierce yet disarming. Her smooth dusky skin was without blemish, and the braids she wore were adorned with sleeves of gold and pins decorated with precious stones.

"No one asked me if I wanted this, Ama. I am only sixteen and yet you act like I am going to rot. I don't even know what Crown Prince Negasi looks like." Sebele retorted. "For all I know he could be as ugly as Temesgen."

Temesgen stuck out his six year old tongue and mimicked a baboon noise at his sister.

"If you ask me, Abbu, Ama, I would be glad to simply get up, stretch my legs and sleep in a real bed without the threat of a pack of hyenas wanting to try their luck. I hate the wilderness." Princess Tigist interjected. "Sebele you should be happy to get married, The Black Seal clan is the only one with more land than our father. A union would make our two clans unstoppable."

"Then you marry him." Sebele replied. "You are clearly shameless enough."

"SEBELE!" Negast Menin was losing her patience. "I will not ask you again. You are a princess of the Black Lion clan, and you will act accordingly. Now quiet or you will wake up Yezina…and put that knife away, do you want them to think that we are barbarians like the Rahisheen?"

"But Ama you didn't ask me, you threatened me with soap." Sebele tucked the sheathed knife into the sash of her kemis. Her mother's firm hand brought across her umber cheek was enough to remind Sebele of her station. The princess rubbed the stinging flesh and continued to speak.

"Yezina is barely four and she sleeps like dead cat, look at her with that mouth open."

Little Yezina was asleep on Prince Fasil's lap. Her mouth was wide open and drooling. Both she and Fasil had been fast asleep since midday prayers, and Sebele hoped they stayed asleep until they arrived at Mah.

Before the queen could respond there was a great horn blast, and the carriage slowed to a halt. The door was opened by one of the royal guards, clad in his crocodile hide cuirass, war sandals and high turban. He put a fist to his chest bowed as Negus Yohannes led his family out of the carriage and into the daylight. The salt smell of the endless waters blew over them. The sound of the waves crashing against the cliffs betrayed their proximity. At about this moment, Sebele wished that she could throw herself over the nearby cliff and let Sunshaia take her away into the sea, but it was too late.

"Peace and blessings be upon you!" Negus Beka called out to his guests.

Negus Beka was a tall and slender man with a grey beard and the hair shorn from the sides of his head. His locks were braided together and hung like a tail down his back. He was missing his left hand, likely cut from his wrist in one of the many battles that bloodied the green fields of the Horn. Even when he smiled his face seemed pinched together, pressed tightly around his slanted black eyes. He was accompanied by his wife and children. Behind them stood their royal guard, their locks hanging from beneath their bronze helms and their faces covered with bronze masks. This matched well with their bronze breastplates and spears, contrasted with the black of their rhino hide shields.

Princess Sebele eyed the lot of them. Each and every one of them, even the queen bore the same small round head and pinched face as their patriarch. They likely wanted her for new blood more than anything else. She eyed Crown Prince Negasi, who spied her as well from the corner of his eye. He was not homely, but he was not comely either. His head was shaven and without locks. He had never drawn blood in battle, and from the look of him, he was old enough to at least have seen a skirmish. She curled her lip in disgust at the thought of having to take a weak husband into her bed.

"Peace and blessings be upon you as well, Negus Beka." Negus Yohannes approached him with open arms.

Negus Beka responded in kind and the two kings embraced one another "I embrace you as my guest, and welcome you to my city. Sunshaia has been merciful to you on your voyage I hope."

"As you can see, we are all in one piece. It is as good to embrace you as an ally as it was an honour to cross swords with you on the field." Negus Yohannes released his grip and nodded respectfully.

Negus Beka nodded in turn. "The honour was and always will be mine. Now mayhap, we shall honour each other with a crossing of our lines instead of our swords. May the wall of enmity be broken in favour of a door of friendship. I present to you here my family, Negast Mesret, Princess Louam, Prince Melaku, and my heir Crown Prince Negasi."

Each of them stepped forward and bowed their heads in respect to Negus Yohannes. In his turn, the negus of Murhad outstretched his arm and introduced his own family.

"I have brought my whole family, my dearest wife, Negast Menin, my eldest, Princess Sebele, Princess Tigist, Crown Prince Temesgen, Prince Fasil, and my youngest, Princess Yezina."

Negus Yohannes' family members each stepped forward and extended the same courtesy as their hosts, save Yezina, who was still asleep in the arms of one of the handmaids.

Negus Beka smiled at them and nodded in acknowledgement. "Please, come Negus Yohannes, there is coffee, dabo, and honey awaiting us in the great hall of my palace. I will have water for you to wash before you enter."

Princess Sebele and her family returned to their carriage and rode through the city gates behind the carriage that bore their hosts. Mah was a beautiful city. The thatch-roofed, conical stone houses were painted in a cornucopia of bright colours, each of them with small gardens and tall fruit trees. Cooking fires filled the air with the smell of coffee, roasted meat, and baking bread. She wondered for a moment if living here wold not be so bad. The Maheen were not so different from the Murhadeen. They were all from the Rahmineen tribe, and making peace with them would please the gods.

The carriage slowed again as it entered the gates to Negus Beka's palace compound. The compound was full of brightly coloured birds, fruit trees, and sweet smelling flowers. She watched the royal guard eye the compound suspiciously. They always eyed everything with suspicion. The carriage came to a halt and the royal family of Murhad disembarked. Flanked by their guards, they entered the palace. Much like the houses and villas of the city, it was brightly painted. The walls came alive with murals of great battles and tales from the ancient days. One of the newer ones seemed to depict Negus Beka hunting a lion at night with a great spear in his good hand.

In the dining hall, they sat cross legged on the floor at a round table where each of them was offered a bowl with lemon and water to wash their hands and face, and another to rinse their mouths. Servants soon came with the coffee, dabo and honey. A man Sebele could only identify as the palace sage from his dress and manner, followed by a pair of novices in white cloaks, circled the room reciting prayers of peace. He waved a bronze censor that vomited forth great clouds of myrrh while the first round of coffee was served. Each of them received a small clay cup and a small saucer filled with honey in which to dip their bread.

The coffee ceremony was an ancient rite shared between the chiefs of old before the great city-states. When they met to trade, negotiate terms of peace, or exchange offspring in marriage, they shared coffee. The offering of coffee, a drink born from the marriage of Sunshadeen and Sunshaia, symbolized a respect for the harmony created by the gods and a desire for peace. One pot of coffee was brewed in the name of each of the gods, first Sun, then Sunshaia, and finally Sunshadeen.

Negus Beka raised his cup. "May the gods bless us and all that we hold dear, that we may enjoy brotherhood in all the years to come."

All in attendance raised their cups and sipped their coffee. It was strong, much more potent than Sebele was used to. The dabo was soft and still warm from the oven. The honey was sweet with a bit of honeycomb in it to add texture.

"Negus Beka, may I praise the richness of your coffee, the softness of your dabo, and the sweetness of your honey." Negus Yohannes continued with the customary pleasantries before it was time to negotiate a dowry.

"All made richer, softer, and sweeter still by the good company of you and your kin." Negus Beka replied.

Sebele found proceedings like these to be tedious. While she loved the fare, the ceremony that went with it had her fighting her near-instinctive eye-roll. The negotiations for her bride price were soon to begin, and she could not wait for them to be over. However, as was the custom in the Horn, they were to last for three days, even if an acceptable offer is made to the bride's family. The second round of coffee came, and the negotiations began.

Negus Beka spoke first, "What then would be acceptable in your sight, O Negus Yohannes, for my son and my clan to be honoured with the hand of your Princess Sebele in marriage? My son will make for her a brave and loyal husband. In anticipation of marriage to your daughter. He has remained untouched by a woman since he expressed his intention to marry her. Shall I give you her weight in gold, five hundred head of sheep, fifty jars of frankincense, fifty jars of myrrh, two hundred jugs of wine, and one hundred of the finest swords?"

Negus Yohannes sucked the honey from his finger before breaking another portion of the dabo for himself. "While I am sure your offer, O Negus Beka, is generous, my daughter is well precious to my clan. She is brave, she is bright, she is loyal, and doubtless she will bear many sons to increase your line. For this I would ask one bull's weight in gold, another bull's weight in bars of bronze, one thousand head of sheep, one hundred jars of frankincense, one hundred jars of myrrh, two hundred jugs of wine, and several hundred of your finest swords."

Sebele discretely squeezed a portion of the bread in her hand. She hated everything about this. She felt like a dumb prized cow in the market square watching two dusty foot farmers haggle over her price, making the number of calves she will bear her main selling point. None of them cared that she loved archery, wrestling, and stick fencing. It did not matter to them that her favourite pastime was galloping through green fields on her horse while Sun smiled on her face in the heat of the midday. No, what mattered to her father and her future father-in-law was her loyalty and capacity for successfully bearing yam-headed children for her yam-headed husband.

They continued back and forth, drinking cup after cup of coffee until dinner was served. Grand platters full of stewed chicken and egg, lamb, sour greens, lentils and injera covered the table top. Through the meal, the two kings exchanged forced pleasantries and debated over Sebele's bride price between bites. Sebele sipped her honey water and strained to keep her mouth quiet as they discussed the rest of her life in front of her.

Having finished dinner, Negus Yohannes called for an end to the first day of negotiations. "O Negus Beka, your hospitality and is welcomed, and I am pleased to see that you place such a high value on my daughter's virtue. Perhaps we have reached an impasse today and should take some time to think on an offer that would be acceptable to both of us?"

Negus Beka rose to his feet and offered Negus Yohannes his hand. The offer was accepted and they embraced again, faces smiling widely.

"So it shall be. Perhaps tomorrow after midday prayers we will sit at this table, and in the sight of our gods and come to an agreement that will honour both of our houses." Negus Beka smiled before turning his face to Sebele. "You will be a most welcome addition to our clan, O Princess Sebele. I only hope that our gift to your father will be enough to compensate him for the loss of you."

Princess Sebele looked at her mother's scowling eyes sitting above a prim smile and looked back at Negus Beka. "I only hope that I can live up to the expectations that my reputation has set for you. I will be a loyal wife to Prince Negasi."

The evening concluded and everyone retired to their chambers. The royal family was attended by their servants in preparations for a long awaited night's sleep. After her servants bathed, oiled and dressed her for bed, Sebele sat on a stool in front of the mirror while one of her handmaids combed and braided her hair. The princess stared into the eyes of her reflection, dark as midnight, as the dancing lamp light flickered against her mahogany face. Her countenance was a gift from her father, and her manner from her mother. She was called beautiful often, though at times she wondered if that was only because she was a princess. Sebele had seen common girls prettier than she, but they would never be compared to her due to their low station.

"I don't want to do this, Selam." Sebele said to her handmaid's reflection. "I will not be happy here."

"If the gods see fit for you to marry the crown prince, who are you to disagree?" The servant chose her words carefully.

"If only it was the gods. My father wants to forge an alliance with the Black Seal clan and is using me to do it. I would rather have married another Black Lion. Our men are strong and handsome. This Crown Prince Negasi is a grown man that hasn't earned his locks yet or even has the decency to greet me or look me directly in the eye." She groaned. "Have you seen that prince? His head looks like a dry yam. I am sure that he is about as intelligent."

Selam snickered as she twisted the last of the braids and began to tie the princess' head with a silk scarf. "Perhaps you will be fortunate to find something more than dirt between the ears of that dry yam."

There was a knock at the door. "Princess, may I speak with you?"

"Go and get the door Selam." Princess Sebele wrapped a shawl over her shoulders and rose from the stool.

Selam walked to the door. "Who is there?"

"Crown Prince Negasi, I would like to speak with the princess."

Selam looked over at the princess. Sebele nodded and motioned for her to open the door.

"How can I help you, O Crown Prince Negasi?" Selam asked.

Sebele listened for an answer, it was a sword point pressing through Selam's belly, running her through and leaving a bloodied hole in the back of her dress.

"SELAM!" She shouted as her handmaid writhed and bled on the floor.

Prince Negasi stepped over the dying servant, the blood dripping from his bronze blade onto the intricate patterns of the rug beneath his sandals. "Your father is dead, your mother is dead, your siblings are dead. Now there is only you. You will be my wife, and I will be your king."

Without hesitation, Sebele grabbed her knife from the dresser and unsheathed it. "Take one step closer and you will be the first man in your family to lose his cock in a fight."

"You really think that you can fight me? You are a woman with a little knife and I have a sword. If you want my cock so badly, you don't have to wait until the wedding night. I can give it to you right now." He stepped forward.

Princess Sebele took the shawl from around her shoulders and wrapped it around her off hand in the way she did when stick fencing. "Come then, we will see if you get to keep it."

As soon as Negasi came within reach, Sebele pounced on him, giving him no time to swing his sword. In an instant, she threw him over her shoulder and on the bed, raising her arm to thrust the knife down at his throat. The strong hand of one of his guards caught her before the knife could come down while the other took hold of her off hand. The guards held her by the arms while Negasi returned to his feet, his pinched face looking uglier than ever.

"You are going to pay for that." He snarled, pushing his face close to hers.

Without a word, she bit his nose with as much force as she could muster, amputating the tip and spitting it back at his face while he shouted in agony, cradling the wound. Sebele started to kick, and writhe, wriggle and wrestle against the iron grip on her wrists. The guards would not let go. Prince Negasi recovered himself and took his sword in hand.

"It would have been easier to rule the Horn with you as my wife, but I can do it in my father's name after you are dead. Goodnight, princess, may the Sunshadeen carry you to Sun's halo swiftly." He drew back his blade and thrust forward.

Just before the blade could land, Sebele jerked herself to the side and brought one of the guards holding her in front of the blade. Negasi's thrust met his henchman's thigh while Sebele's teeth met the fingers of her other captor. As soon as their hands released her wrists, she pushed Negasi aside, skipped over the bed and climbed up the windowsill.

She looked down and saw the crashing waves of the sea beating against the rocks below. She muttered a prayer to Sunshaia and prepared to jump. Negasi and his men came for her, reaching out to pull her back into the palace. She leaned out of the window, and whispered to herself. "May Sunshaia have mercy on you, because I will not."

Without another word, Sebele threw herself head first into the Sunshaia's embrace, trusting her life to the endless waters and the goddess' protection.

A Gift from the Gods

The waves lapped gently against the white sands where the princess slept. Waterlogged and exhausted, she lay sprawled on the beach with the sea rising just below her chin, as if Sunshaia was covering her in a blanket while she slept. It was late morning, and Sun had shone over her, trying to wake her with light since painting the sky many hours ago. Still, she slept.

When she plunged into the sea the night before, the impact against the surface nearly winded her, and then the waves swallowed her. In the absence of the moon, the stars alone did not provide sufficient light for her to find her bearings by sight. Tossed around by the rising tide, and unable to see the direction of the shoreline, Sebele was left with little recourse but to swim by sound and follow the crash of the waves against the stones below the cliff. Sunshaia was merciful and did not allow the sea to shatter Sebele's bones upon them. The waves washed her gently against them, and like the gentle hands of a caring mother, guided her past them until she came to the beach. When she felt the sand beneath her feet, the princess dragged herself ashore like a sea turtle about to lay her eggs. However, Sebele did not come ashore to bring life. In her belly grew the desire for vengeance, and vengeance she would have.

The sea pushed her up the beach again, and feeling the hot sand against her skin, Princess Sebele opened her eyes and gasped. She threw herself on her side and coughed. Her hair was tangled with seaweed and her nightgown was soaked. Her mouth was filled with the taste of the sea. Her muscles were sore, and her heart was broken. Sunshaia had indeed been merciful and did not let her drown. She sat up and whispered a prayer of gratitude to the water goddess.

When the shock of having survived the night had subsided, the grief of losing her family set in. Her mother, her father, her brothers, and her sisters had all perished. She could only imagine the horror by which they were dispatched. Tears came, and a sea of lamentation flowed forth from her eyes. She gripped the sand and wailed her anguish to the heavens and the seas. Visions of their faces flashed in her mind's eye. She lay on her side and cried as she remembered them. Then she remembered Crown Prince Negasi, and his father Negus Beka, and her sorrow turned to rage. She gritted her teeth, and forced herself to stand. Her legs were weak and bent like saplings beneath her, but she held her ground and refused to fall.

"Sun! Sunshaia! Sunshadeen!" She faced the sea and called out to the sky. "The Black Seal clan has violated the pledge of peace they made by blessing coffee and breaking bread with us in YOUR name! Grant me vengeance! Grant me vengeance and I will be your swift and unfaltering hand of judgement against them! I will slaughter them all in your names! Grant me strength and I will visit upon them a maelstrom of woe, the likes of which they have never seen! Help me restore my clan's honour!"

The gods did not speak back. The gods never spoke. It was their way. Sebele sighed and turned towards the land. She would not find her vengeance here. She would need an army, and one was waiting for her across Burning River in the land of Murhad. All she had to do was return to the city of her forefathers and call the people to arms in the name of their slain king and queen. They would sweep through Negus Beka's land like a plague of locusts and lay waste all that stood in their path. However, Sebele needed to make her way to the city gates before the first blade could be drawn. Sebele took her first step towards vengeance, but was stopped by something under her feet. Three oysters seemed to have appeared from thin air, next to the knife she thought she had lost in the sea. Without hesitation she took her knife in hand, and one by one, she shucked the oysters open and consumed the meat, silencing the grumbling in her stomach. The gods have answered. It would be a long walk through the Green Sea and it would be fraught with danger. Sebele knew this, and it did not deter her. She needed her late father's army. She put one foot in front of the other and began her long trek north to Murhad.

From the safety of her carriage, the Green Sea was beautiful. The tall grass danced in the breeze while majestic animals strolled between the swaying blades. Now, out in the open and without the protection of her carriage or the royal guards, she was at the mercy of tooth, claw, and horn. Though her mind raced with the possibility of becoming some wild animal's next target, her heart knew the gods would protect her. By the end of the first day of walking, she was unsure of how far she had gone, but the sight and smell of the rolling sea had passed, exchanged for the rolling hills of the Green Sea.

On her first night in the wilderness, she found a tall acacia tree. With her knife gripped firmly in her teeth, she climbed to the highest branches that would support her weight. She tied her sleeves together around one of the branches and gave in to an uneasy sleep. Throughout the night, she was roused by the howling, groaning, and tittering of the wild. Beneath her, she could hear the steps of something large circling the tree, then the sound of claws digging into the wood accompanied by the groan of an urge to stretch satisfied. She silently prayed that remaining quiet and motionless would keep her safe. The fear of that moment kept her awake for the rest of the night, fearful that a lapse in alertness would mean her end. She watched Sun paint the sky again with the coming of the dawn. Princess Sebele had survived the first day.

The next morning, when danger appeared to have found something more interesting to follow, Princess Sebele slowly lowered herself from the tree and looked around. Without further hesitation, she girded the hem of her nightgown and found herself a stick to sharpen. She would need a walking stick on her journey and a sharp point to deter anyone or anything that would wish to do her harm. She settled on a dry, crooked branch that had fallen from the tree some time ago. Sitting in the shade she sharpened the end as best she could with her knife. It was not a knife made for woodworking, which made the task that much more difficult. That did not stop her. With each shaving of wood she stripped from the point she imagined cutting another strip of flesh from Negus Beka and his yam-headed son. She imagined the screams let out by her mother as they murdered her, the crying of Temesgen, and the wailing of little Yezina. Tears came again. She shook her head and swallowed them back. This was not the time for tears. There would be plenty of time to cry when her family was avenged.

She admired the makeshift spear and tested the point with her thumb for sharpness. This was no bronze spear point, but it would serve for now. Soon she would return with a sea of spears and drown the Black Seal clan in blood.

Sebele rose to her feet, turned north, and began to walk through the waist-high blades of lush grass. She was unsure of how long she walked. She did not bother to count the days. Occasionally she would find some nuts or berries, but it being the middle of the dry season, there was little to eat. Her stomach griped for hunger. Her spear was useless for throwing, and she never learned to hunt, though now she wished she had gone with her father on his expeditions in search of wild meat. She loved to eat the roast antelope, wildebeest, or kudu that he would bring home. He would always carry the carcasses triumphantly on his shoulders, beating his chest and bragging about his prowess as a hunter. She chuckled. She missed her father, and she was sure that the news, once it reached Murhad, would be met with sorrow of equal measure. Her uncle Iskander would call for war. Her father's First Minister Afewerek would echo the call. Lord Tadesse, the master war, would mount his war elephant and shout for the drums of vengeance. Sebele imagined herself riding with them, her war bow in hand on the back of her horse, armoured and ready for battle.

Lost in her daydream, she forgot to pay attention to her surroundings, and nearly stumbled on a pack of wild dogs tearing apart the carcass of a black buffalo they had just killed. She quickly threw herself down on her belly and watched. Despite the gruesome display of splayed entrails and bloody muzzles, her hungry belly called out for just a pound of that flesh. She counted the number of dogs, perhaps she could have chased them off. Thirty, there were too many. She would have to wait. She pressed herself as close to the ground as she could and prayed that the smell of the blood from their kill and the sound of their own chewing would keep her hidden. She silently mouthed a prayer to Sunshadeen in the hopes that the wild dogs would finish eating and go. It seemed that their massive kill was not enough to sate them. They kept eating and Sebele kept praying, gripping her knife and makeshift spear tightly.

She felt something cold sliding over the skin of her spear hand. Sebele opened her eyes and looked for the source of the sensation. What she saw was the body of the longest cobra she had ever seen. She bit her lip and tried not to startle it. Hopefully, the same strategy would work on the snake; however, the snake took too long to pass. Sebele could no longer hold her breath and emptied her lungs. The sudden gust of air startled the snake. It reared up, spread its hood and hissed at her.

Without a second thought, she shot up, and grabbing the snake by the neck, swung it over her head and hurled it among the wild dogs before running for her life. She heard the dogs chirp, snarl, and give chase. She gritted her teeth and pressed forward, fighting through the soreness of her limbs. She scanned the horizon for a tree, a bush, some water, something to help her escape them. There was nothing but green grass in front of her, and frothing death behind her. There was no choice, she had to turn and fight before running left her too exhausted to take at least one dog with her.

Sebele turned on her heels and instead of running from the pack of wild dogs, ran at them with her knife raised, roaring as she charged. If they were going to kill her and leave her thirst for revenge unquenched, Sebele would be sure to make them earn it. As she charged against them, the wild dogs suddenly stopped in their tracks and ran back to the carcass.

The princess halted her advance, and held her knife aloft and panted. "I am Princess Sebele bnit Yohannes! Daughter of the Black Lion clan! I have no fear! You will not keep me from my vengeance!"

Holding her head high, Princess Sebele looked to the sky to gauge Sun's position and find North. She had to cross Burning River. As she turned with her eyes to the sky, she felt the same presence that shook the tree she slept in on her first night. Her blood ran cold. Sebele turned looked over her shoulder, and the presence revealed itself. Standing above her was her clan's namesake with fiery yellow eyes, black regal mane, and shoulders the height of fully grown man.

The great lion stood motionless, his proud ebony tresses dancing the breeze of the Green Sea. Sebele was awestruck, whether it was the sheer beauty of the creature, or the power of his presence, she could not tell. Her mouth was dry, her hands were moist, and her knees were weak. She tried to speak the fire god's name, but her voice had left her, then blackness.

She awoke with a gasp and opened her eyes to a canopy of stars. Night had fallen. Her head was swimming, and her stomach still growled for hunger. She rubbed her eyes and sat up blinking into the darkness, trying to get her bearings. The swollen moon above granted the grass around her a pale glow. There were no trees or rock formations to climb. She was out in the open, exposed and alone. She felt for her knife. It was gone. Hyenas whooped in the distance. She clenched her fist and prepared to die.

"You are awake." A voice echoed in her head. "Your kind is wont to sleep at night."

Sebele leaped to her feet and turned in circles. "Who said that?"

"You are brave, Sunshadeen was right to send us to you."

The voice said again. "You named your pride for us, why?"

The princess was certain that she had gone mad. "Get out of my head! GET OUT OF MY HEAD!" she shouted, grabbing handfuls of her now frayed hair.

"Quiet now, princess, the hyenas will hear you, and unlike us, they will not come to protect you." The voice was calm and steady like that of a grandfather.

She heard the grass bending beneath the footfalls of something large, and nearby.

"Who are you?" She asked, doing her utmost to mask her terror.

The footfalls came closer, and into her field of vision came that same lion that stood over her when the dogs tucked tail and ran. Though his mouth did not move, he spoke: "You may call me Yihuda. I am the first of this pride. You must be Sebele."

"How did you know my name?" She stepped backwards, maintaining eye contact with the lion.

"You shouted it at the wild dogs when you thought you had run them off." Yihuda's voice echoed.

Sebele wrung her hands. "Why can I hear you? Am I dead?"

"If you had died, I would have eaten you and returned you to the soil." The great lion jested as he lay down. "You live, for the gods have heard your plea and will grant you the vengeance you seek for the sacrilege committed by the Black Seal clan."

"Will you kill them for me then?" She asked.

"We will kill no one for you princess." A lioness brushed past Sebele and dropped something at her feet. "We are to keep you alive until you return home, then the rest is up to you."

"Thank you." Sebele bowed her head. "And thank the gods for sending you to me. What is your name?"

"You may call me Eddel." The lioness replied before fading into the darkness.

"Now eat." Yihuda pointed to Sebele's feet with his nose. "You will need strength for the rest of this journey."

Sebele reached down and found the largest pomegranate she had ever eaten in her life. Without a moment's hesitation, she tore into it with her teeth in a manner not unlike the way the wild dogs had torn into that buffalo. The flesh was sweet, but not as sweet as her revenge would be.

Pride and Power

Sebele walked along with the lions, keeping up the pace as best she could. She did not trust the looks of the lionesses and their cubs, so she made a concerted effort to stay close to Yihuda. Their strides were long, and they covered the ground quickly. For several days they walked through the swaying grasses. The lions hunted and shared a kill each day. For the first few days, she would watch them eat while she searched any nearby bushes or trees for fruit. There were none. Though she had never eaten raw meat, her hunger made it an appetizing prospect. Eventually, she gave in and one bite at a time, Sebele would silence her griping belly with a few mouthfuls of the kills the lions made. While she waited for the lions to sleep off their meals, Sebele would find ways to occupy her time. She learned how to make a hand axe from stone, and even used it to fashion herself another pointed walking stick from a young tree.

The long walk, however, was beginning to take its toll on her body. Sebele was a princess. Her feet were accustomed to silk slippers and sandals made from the softest lamb leather. Her skin was oiled and perfumed daily. Her hair was always combed and braided. Her stomach was accustomed to fine stews, sweet steamed greens, and gravy-soaked injera. The wilderness had none of this. Her feet were blistered and bleeding. She had taken her braids out. Her hair was matted and full of grass and dirt. Her fine princess' nightgown was soiled and torn. Her stomach burned with hunger. She looked every bit the lowly beggar. Yet despite all of the pain, the hunger, and the indignity of having to relieve herself in the company of animals, Sebele still carried herself with pride. Neither dirt, nor hunger, nor indignity would make her forget herself. With each painful step, she continued to walk with her head high. There would be plenty of time for tears when her vendetta was settled.

"Look at her, she can barely keep up." Eddel remarked to one of the other lionesses. "If she can't make the journey home, what hope has she of avenging her kin?"

"Pay my daughter no mind, O Princess." Yihuda's voice echoed in Sebele's head. "The gods have dictated that vengeance shall be yours."

"What makes you so sure that I will succeed?" Sebele asked.

"You should have died many times over out here. We watched you since the coast. There are dangers out here that your eye is not trained to see, nor your ear to hear. You knew those wild dogs would finish you if they caught you. Yet, you ran towards them because you wanted to fight for your life. It is valuable to you; there is fire in your veins."

Sebele listened carefully. She had never known that animals possessed such wisdom. Her grandmother would tell her tales of deceitful spiders, clever monkeys and ill-tempered bush pigs, but she always took them for fables. They were animals, just roaming, eating, killing, and running as was the way of the wild. Yihuda showed her that there was more to them than the savagery of the wilderness. There was quiet nobility to their lives. The lions, though they had the power to rule their world with a bronze claw, never took more than they needed to survive. They had no natural predators, save the men that hunted them for their manes. Yihuda explained that if they chased every animal they saw, they would kill everything and then starve for want of game. The combination of their power and restraint earned them respect.

The hyenas, however, were different. Not a living thing could pass their noses without a frenzy of snapping jaws and yowling. They did not even wait until their prey was dead before they ate it. The thought of being eaten alive sent a chill down Sebele's spine. After that revelation, very little was said, and they walked in silence. The quiet of their sojourn was interrupted by Eddel.

"Buffalo! Everyone down!"

The pride immediately dropped to their bellies. Sebele did the same. With her muzzle, Eddel pointed out a herd comprised of a motley assemblage of horned beasts gathered at the edge of Burning River, drinking and grazing. With her eyes, Eddel gave the order, and the lionesses split in their various directions, leaving Sebele to sit with Yihuda and the cubs.

"You wish you could go with them?" Yihuda stretched out on his back, exposing his belly to Sun's light as the cubs climbed over and around him.

"My father loved to hunt. I never went with him." Sebele sat on the ground, a cub curled up and half-sleeping on her lap.

"You yaheen[22] are strange. You send your men out to hunt, when you have women that are more than capable of doing it." Yihuda yawned as one of the cubs playfully nibbled at his ear.

"You could say that, you could also say that you lions like to sleep too much." Sebele winked.

Her retort garnered no reaction. Yihuda had fallen asleep, one cub gnawing at his ear while another chased the tuft at the end of his flicking tail.

Sebele sighed, and watched the lionesses hunt in the distance. Though she could not see their bodies, she saw the grass part around them as they formed a semi-circle around the herd. They took their time, moving slowly and deliberately towards their target. The grass

---

[22] Humans/Mankind

stopped. Sebele counted to three under her breath, and the chase was on. Eddel sprung out first and swiped at the hindquarters of an old buffalo. She missed on purpose, driving him forward. Then, another of the lionesses, sprung forward, chasing the massive beast in another direction. When the old buffalo changed directions, two more lionesses sprang out of the grass and pounced on him. One had her massive jaws around his neck, and the other two at his hind legs while the rest stood back and watched.

In an instant the buffalo fell screaming, then, with a twist of her body, the lioness silenced the buffalo and quenched his divine fire.

"The food is ready your majesty." Sebele said to Yihuda, whose ears perked up at the promise of a meal.

He licked his nose and rolled back onto his belly. "Come now children, time to eat. You know your father gets the first bite, and those hind quarters are looking thick and delicious."

"How can you tell from this far?" Sebele asked.

"The hind quarters are always thick and delicious. Come now Sebele, you only nibble at the kill; you have yet to try the best meat."

The princess shook the cub in her lap awake and rose to her feet, taking her new walking stick in hand. She was always perplexed by the way the lions ate. The lionesses would do all of the work and chase the meat, but it was Yihuda who always ate first. Eddel said once that it was his payment for protecting the cubs, which they valued above all else.

As they approached the kill, that terrifying whoop that she always heard echoing in the distance went up again. This time, it was no echo. Princess Sebele looked to Yihuda, who raised his head and scanned the distance.

"Take the cubs to the lionesses, now."

Without a moment's hesitation, Sebele called to the cubs and they began to run through the grass toward the lionesses. "Hyenas! Hyenas!"

"Guard the kill, I will get the cubs!" Eddel told the other lionesses.

The young lioness ran to Sebele and picked up one of the cubs by the scruff with her teeth. Sebele would have loved to help by carrying one herself, but they were almost the same size as her. The whooping continued, followed by yowling. The voices increased in number. Terror set in.

Just as Sebele, Eddel, and the cubs arrived at the kill, the first hyena emerged from the tall grass. He was thin and ungainly looking, with black eyes and half of his ear missing. He bore his teeth and yowled again before several others of his kind appeared behind him.

"Protect the cubs and the kill!" Eddel repeated her command.

Sebele and the cubs took up a place behind the lionesses, which formed a semi-circle around the cubs and buffalo carcass. More hyenas arrived, each one looking hungrier than the last. Their number continued to increase. They were outnumbered. The hyenas began to whoop and yowl again, spreading themselves out and slowly approaching the lionesses, who hissed, growled, and gnashed their teeth. There were so many of them, even more than the number of wild dogs that had chased Sebele when she met the lions. The cubs were terrified.

Sebele held her walking stick tightly, prepared to fight for her life. The hyenas came closer, snapping their jaws at the lionesses, testing for fear and weakness. Every time they came into reach, the lionesses would swipe at them with their dagger-like claws. The hyenas never came close enough, but their numbers continued to increase. When it seemed like every hyena in the Green Sea had come out of the grass, and were ready to attack.

"Yihuda! Yihuda! Where are you?" Sebele called out to her protector.

He was nowhere to be seen. This, however, did not mean that he was not present. Like some great storm cloud, Yihuda sprang from the tall grass and unleashed his fury upon the hyenas. They scattered beneath him in confusion, not knowing whether to attack, run, or watch. Yihuda wasted no time. He broke their backs betwixt his colossal jaws, nearly snapping them in half like dry twigs. He had killed or disabled at least six of them before the hyenas gathered themselves and counterattacked. Eddel charged forward to help her father, followed by a few of the lionesses.

Despite their numerical advantage, the hyenas found themselves being thrown down one after another before the great lions. Sebele was awestruck by the savagery of the engagement. Blood, fur, urine, and feces littered the battlefield to the sound of a cacophony of roaring, hissing, growling, and yelping. It seemed that the number of hyenas was only increasing. More of them emerged from the grass and bypassed Yihuda, Eddel, and the other lionesses entirely. Their sights were set on the buffalo carcass, the cubs, and Sebele.

The lionesses left to guard Sebele and the cubs charged forward, tearing into the flesh of their attackers, and suffering severe bites of their own. There were so many of them. The first of the lionesses fell under the jaws of so many hyenas that all that could be seen of her was the blood and flesh thrown in the air by her attackers.

Sebele's heart pounded in terror, but she would not be moved. The gods promised her vengeance, and no pack of hyenas would take that from her.

"All glory to Sunshadeen!" she shouted as she charged at the first hyena to make eye contact.

He came at her with his gaping, bloody muzzle. The princess scowled and rammed the point of her walking stick down the hyena's throat. The animal thrashed and struggled, but she held on, pressing forward until he lost his balance. As soon as the beast was down, she grabbed hold of the largest stone she could find, and threw it down upon his head, breaking the skull and ending his life. She pulled her stick out of his mouth; it was wet with blood and bile.

The cubs were shrieking. Despite their size, the cubs were still young and did not know how to fight off an attacker. The hyenas that were not already eating the buffalo carcass had started to tear the cubs to shreds. Sebele raised her stick and attacked, bellowing her war cry from the depths of her belly. She forced the semi-blunt tip of her stick into the ribs of the nearest hyena to her. She pressed so hard, the bluntness of her weapon was no obstacle to her planting it deep into the animal's chest, killing him instantly. Before she could yank it out and choose another target, she was pulled to the ground by the tattered ends of her nightgown and was soon mounted by one of the hyenas. It snapped at her face. She braced her forearm against its neck to keep the teeth away from her throat and drove the thumb from her free hand into its eye. The hyena backed away and gave her just enough time to find another stone and beat it about the head until death claimed it as well.

By the time she had managed to slay that last hyena, all of the cubs were dead or dying with their entrails being devoured by their assailants. Sebele looked around her and saw that despite their best efforts, and mounting piles of dead and dying hyenas, the lions were going to lose.

"Eddel!" Yihuda roared. "You must away with the princess!"

"No!" Eddel replied as she shook and threw another hyena. "Father, I will not leave you! You are our lion, you must protect the cubs!"

"The cubs are dead! GO!" Yihuda ordered his daughter.

Eddel ran over to Sebele, narrowly evading the snapping jaws of their enemies. "Come! On my back, NOW!" She bowed her head.

Sebele did as she was told and climbed on to Eddel's back. She gripped handfuls of her midnight fur and held on for dear life as the lioness ran for the same.

"What about Yihuda?" Sebele asked.

"He told me to take you, and take you is what I will do. Sunshadeen has commanded my father, and my father has commanded me." Eddel replied.

Sebele looked over her shoulder to see her protector continuing to cut the hyenas apart as they surrounded him while the other lionesses began to break and run after her and Eddel.

"We can't leave him! He will die!" Sebele shouted, tears in her eyes. "He saved my life."

"He saved your life, but he gave me mine." Eddel replied.

Sebele and the lionesses threw themselves into the river, despite the danger of crocodiles and kibokeen. The risk was worth it. The hyenas did not follow them into the water, instead they returned to the feast and the battle. As the lionesses swam for their lives to the opposite bank, Sebele could see the fatigued Yihuda, the great black lion, fighting until he was finally enveloped by the horde of ravenous jaws, disappearing forever.

<u>Something Foul</u>

They marched toward the city gates in silence, the horror of the hyena attack still fresh in their minds so many days later. After the carnage of the encounter, there remained only a handful of survivors, some of them grievously wounded. Yihuda was gone, the cubs were gone, and so were most of the lionesses. Sunshaia was merciful and saw them across Burning River unmolested, though badly shaken. In the final days of their trek, the most injured among them succumbed to their wounds and gave up to the gods their divine fire. There was little to eat, and though they did not starve, the pangs of emptiness in their bellies stung at them as frustration wore on.

Eddel continued to bear Sebele on her back. The blisters on the princess' feet burst and bled. Walking had become too painful. Sebele's heart was heavy, and she knew that Eddel's was as well. Eddel did not speak, not even of the grief she felt for her father.

"There is Murhad." Princess Sebele pointed to the city as they reached the top of another hill.

The city sat high on a hill in the distance. The tiny farming settlements just outside of the city walls were alive with fires, livestock, and farmers pacing in their fields. The princess closed her eyes and said a silent prayer of thanks to the gods for bringing her so far.

Eddel sniffed the air "I will carry you to the outskirts, then we will leave you and return to the wild. You yaheen are not always welcoming to us when we stray near your territory, though you venture into ours often."

"Eddel, you and your pride will always be welcome within the walls of Murhad." Sebele scratched the lioness' ear. "When I sit the throne that was my father's you will have an honoured place among us. We will feed you the fattest lambs, and there will be no hyenas to murder your cubs."

"We shall see." Eddel lead the pride down the hill and towards the city.

When they arrived, the farmers gasped and ran in terror. Some pulled their animals into their stables; others pulled their children inside and shut the doors. The rest ran into the city shouting that there was a wild woman astride a great black lioness and coming into the city. Bells rang and horns blasted. The sudden urgent clamour gave some of the lionesses pause to go any further. Eddel was not deterred, and continued towards the gate.

"I thought you were going to leave and let me walk to the gate?" Sebele smiled.

The lioness looked back at her. "The reception was far less hostile than I expected. I have never been inside of a yaheen city. I want to see what is past that gate."

"And perhaps some fat lambs?" Sebele smiled. "Come, my uncle will be -"

The princess stopped short of finishing her sentence as a contingent of well-armed men on their striped horses came barrelling out of the city gates, their lances and bows in hand.

"Who comes here uninvited in the company of beasts to the city of Negus Iskander?" The captain asked, lance pointed at the princess.

Sebele pushed her matted tresses back to expose her face. Her eyes looked on them, hot as fire. "Your true negast, Sebele bnit Yohannes."

"You lie!" The captain snarled. "The royal family was slaughtered by bandits in the wilderness. You are a mad woman. Be gone! You and your lions will leave this city."

"I don't think they believe you." Eddel's voice echoed in the princess' head.

Sebele would not be deterred. "How dare you question the righteousness of my claim? Look on me. LOOK ON ME! I am Sebele bnit Yohannes, daughter of the Black Lion clan! I was born in the walls of this city! My father, my mother, my brothers and my sisters were slain by bandits yes, but by bandits that live in the palace of Mah that wear fine silks and spit on declarations of peace at the feet of the gods! I have borne witness to horrors that live only in your nightmares. I have come to claim my place on the throne, and I have come to call you to arms! Honour must be satisfied, and we must seek revenge!"

The captain looked to his men. "Get her out of here."

They followed their orders and advanced on the princess. Eddel snarled at them and bore her dagger-like teeth. The horses refused to take another step.

"You, what is your name?" Sebele demanded.

"Captain Gebre."

"Captain Gebre, if you doubt me, then I have a proof for you. Go and call First Minister Afewerek or Lord Tadesse, or any of their kin. They will know me." The princess said.

The captain smirked and cocked his head to the side. "And if they do not know you, what shall be done with you?"

"Then I will leave." She replied.

"That will not be enough for me, especially for the waste of my precious time." He smirked and licked his lips. "I will find some way for you to serve me in exchange for my time, and that of my men."

Sebele curled her upper lip in disgust. "Fine, go and bring them here. When I am proven, then you will compensate me for the loss of my time."

"And what compensation will you require?" The captain leaned forward in his saddle.

"I will find a way." She replied. "Now send your man."

The captain looked over his shoulder and clicked his tongue at one of his men, who turned his horse and rode back into the city.

"Are you sure that they will recognize you?" Eddel's voice whispered in the princess' mind.

Sebele stroked her neck. "Trust me."

A few moments later a well-dressed man came forward, tall and stately. His grey beard was thick and his silk overcoat shimmered in Sun's light. He was carried through the city gates on a sedan chair, borne by a group of tall male servants.

"Down." He waved his hand.

The servants did as they were told, and the man rose to his feet. "Captain Gebre, where is this miscreant that claims to be our dear Princess Sebele?"

"See her here, O First Minister." The captain chuckled.

He stepped forward between the horses and stood before Princess Sebele and Eddel.

"You are not the First Minister." Princess Sebele's blood began to boil.

The man protested. "I certainly am the First Minister, I knew the negus and his family well. You cannot tell me that I do not."

"I know your face Sage Brehan. You pulled me from my mother when I broke water, and you tended me when I nearly died of fever two monsoons ago." She spat back. "That you would come and insult me by taking part in this farce has broken my heart. How could you?"

The man blinked. He turned his head sideways and looked on the princess with eyes that now seriously considered her claim. He looked through the dirt and matted hair. He saw past her tattered clothes. He ignored the wild smells of sweat and grass that replaced the perfumes that once sweetened her flesh. He fell to his knees and bowed before her.

"All glory to the gods! It is her! It is Princess Sebele!" He exclaimed.

The captain and the guards looked shocked, and then afraid.

"You are not serious, O First Minister, she is a wild woman, she is mad!" Captain Gebre's voice was trembling.

"Give it up, Captain Gebre, she knows who I am, and it is her. It is her!" Sage Brehan rose to his feet, his wizened face smiling as the princess had never seen before. "Bring her in, bring her in immediately! Bring the chair! The princess is home!"

The servants immediately raised the sedan chair on their shoulders and presented it to her. The captain and his men still looked on, their jaws hanging in disbelief.

"No, I will enter the city on the back of my lioness, followed by those behind me. They have guarded me in the wilderness and they will come with me. They will be given comfort in the stables and fed the fattest lambs we have until their hunger is sated." Princess Sebele declared. "And you, Captain Gebre, you will serve me yet. Bow your head and go announce to the people that their negast has come, and war will follow."

"Yes, O Princess. The captain bowed his head. His men followed suit.

Without another word, they all turned and led the princess in to the city, blowing their horns to proclaim her arrival. The people that ran from her when she arrived came out to peek around corners and through windows at the princess who returned from the dead on the back of a black lioness. They watched silently as she and Eddel lead the nervous pride of lionesses through the gates and into the city behind the warriors of Murhad.

"All hail Princess Sebele!" A jubilant voice broke the silence, and then cheering began.

Sebele had returned home in triumph. He held her matted head high and rode her lioness through the city streets. The first leg of her journey was complete.

"Eddel, I will take you to the stables where you and the others can sleep. You will each be given the fattest sheep in the royal herd. They will be slaughtered and skinned for you." Sebele said.

"Thank you." Eddel replied.

"Sage Brehan, where is my uncle?"

"He is having his midday meal, O Princess." He replied. "His heart will be gladdened to know that you have returned."

Sebele could not help but wonder if it would be so. The laws of succession made her the queen and rendered her uncle's claim to the throne moot. Once a crown is placed on a man's head, it is not dislodged so easily.

The lionesses were given their accommodations after all of the horses had been removed from one of the royal stables and spread out between the others. Sebele was brought to the palace on a sedan chair, where she was bathed by servants, had her bloodied feet tended and her hair cleaned and braided. Her skin was oiled and perfumed. Her tattered rags were replaced with a brilliant white kemis of fine linen, trimmed with gold thread and dyed wool. On her neck she wore gold chains adorned with opals, lapis lazuli, pearls and rubies. She was fed hot lamb stew and injera, washing it down with all of the honey water that she could drink. It had been so long since she had tasted cooked meat. While she learned to tolerate the bloody flesh of a fresh kill, it could never match the flavour of a savoury stew and hot bread.

As she ate, Sebele's mind ran wild with fantasies of her revenge. She would assemble the largest army that Murhad had ever produced, and she would lead them across the Green Sea and into Mah. The negus of Mah and his entire family would die screaming. She eyed her war bow and quiver that hung from the wall, and imagined loosing arrow after arrow into Negus Beka's head and chest. Negus Beka's men would fall like droplets of rain and their blood would flood the battlefield. Prince Negasi would be relieved of the rest of his extremities, and the entire city of Mah would be laid to waste. To accomplish this feat, she would need her strength, and so she ate, finishing her meal with a pomegranate and licking the juice from her fingers. There was a knock at the door.

"Princess Sebele." Said one of the palace guards. "Negus Iskander will see you now."

"I come." She rose to her feet, washed her hands, and headed for the door.

Negus Iskander sat on her father's throne, flanked by First Minister Afewerek and Lord Tadesse. He looked every bit the king, his head held high, swathed in fine robes and gold chains. His beard had been trimmed since she last saw him. His locks were neatly braided together and hung low over his shoulders. In his hand he held the sceptre of chiefdom, a golden rod with a roaring lion's head. After her time in the wilderness, the image took on a completely different meaning.

"Uncle." She bowed her head and greeted him.

Negus Iskander rose from his seat and handed the sceptre to Afewerek. He stepped down from the royal dais and opened his arms. "Sebele, daughter of my beloved brother. Come and embrace your uncle." They embraced each other, and he kissed her forehead. "I thought you slaughtered in the wilderness. Sunshaia has delivered you home."

Sebele began to weep "Uncle, we must revenge our family."

"My niece, we will send warriors to scour the Green Sea and put those bandits under the sword." He declared. "Then we will find you a proper husband from Murad as your father should have chosen."

Sebele stepped backwards. "Who told you this lie?"

"What lie, Sebele?"

"My father, mother, and all of my siblings, down to little Yezina, were slaughtered in the palace of Negus Beka." She said. "They tried to kill me. I was thrown into the wilderness with neither tooth nor claw nor sword. I was chased by wild dogs, fought with hyenas, and still I returned to the city gates on the back of a lioness. I want revenge uncle. I want Negus Beka and his entire ill-bred stock put to the point of a spear and slaughtered." Her eyes were wildfire. The memory of that night filled her with a rage that burned hotter than Sunshadeen's Mouth.

Iskander crossed his arms. "My niece, you have given me much to ponder. Captain Tedros himself brought news of your demise. How are you sure that it was Negus Beka?"

Sebele clenched her fist and swallowed the urge to shake her uncle back to his senses. "I know because Prince Negasi came for me himself. When his men held me by my arms for him, I bit the end of his nose off and spat the blood into his eye. I jumped out of the window and gave myself to Sunshaia, who placed me on the beach and set my foot on the path to this throne room. Uncle, they tried to kill me, and they murdered our kin, your own brother. Why are you not wild with rage? Why do you not beat your chest and tear your garment? Why do you not shake your locks and scream for justice? Where is Tedros? I need to ask him why he would lie! He should be hung the traitor!"

"A king must keep his countenance temperate. Rage is best saved for the battlefield." He placed a hand on her shoulder.

"Captain Tedros died of his wounds shortly after returning to Murhad on the back of his horse, alone and weather-beaten."

This was a lie. Sebele read it in her uncle's face. Something told her that she was not safe here.

Sebele took her uncle's hands in her own. "Uncle, perhaps my time in the wild has filled my head with fantasies of betrayal. Someone must recompense us for the murder of our family. Will you send men to find those bandits?"

Negus Iskander embraced her again, pulling her to his breast. "It will be done. I will dispatch horsemen in the morrow with a description that you will give them, and those brigands will be hunted to the ends of the earth."

"Thank you." She sighed. "I am weary, I think it is best that I go and sleep, for it has been long since my skin felt the kiss of fine linens."

Negus Iskander kissed his niece on the forehead again. "Go then. I shall see you in the morrow."

The princess bowed her head and returned to her chamber under guard. When her door was locked from the outside, she knew that her time would soon come. Without a second thought, she bound her braids and found clothes more fitting for an escape. Perhaps she could go north across the sea to Faldid Island, or further north to the city states of Puntia. It didn't matter where she went, what mattered was that she escaped, soon.

She searched her room, dressing in more rugged clothes for travel, and slipping her riding sandals and a pair of short breeches under her skirt. She threw some clothes in a bag and pulled her war bow and quiver from the wall. Then she waited. As Sun painted the sky and day gave way to evening, she prayed to the gods to make swift her flight. Her revenge would have to wait, for it would not be possible if she were not alive to take it. As darkness overtook the sky and the stars sang their silent melodies to one another, she looked out the window and scanned for an escape route. She would need to make it to the stables to collect Eddel and the other lionesses.

Below her was a balcony several floors down, below that was another, and then finally a cartfull of hay that had come to the palace compound, but not yet gone to the royal stables. Sebele whispered a prayer to the water goddess for protection, and began her escape.

She carefully slid herself out of the window. Without the sea to catch her, she would have to land on her feet, and with much care so as not to break them. First one leg, than the other, then she turned and slowly lowered herself, her belly against the wall. She took three breaths.

"All glory to the gods." Then she let go.

Her feet hit the limestone, and her knees bent in just the right way to keep her silent and stay any injury from such a drop. She repeated the first three steps as she lowered herself to the second balcony. First one leg, then the other, then she turned and slowly lowered her body. She would have to swing her legs to reach the balcony below her instead of falling straight into the hay. She swung her legs and slowly built up momentum.

"Did you hear what the princess said to Negus Iskander?" A voice spoke from below her. It was a palace guard.

"No what?" Said the voice of another guard.

"Negus Yohannes was murdered with the rest of the royal family. I heard it with my own ears from outside of the throne room."

"I thought they was murdered by bandits."

"Yes of course, in the same way that Captain Tedros was beheaded for abandoning Negus Yohannes."

I knew it. The princess thought to herself.

She knew what she had to do. Her uncle was covering a lie, and he had to be exposed. She would leave Murhad, and she would travel north. She would build an army of mercenaries and find new allies. She would return and take the crown for herself, and then she would march that army across the river and lay waste to Negus Beka and all that he held dear. First, she needed to escape.

Her fingertips trembled as she tried to hold her grip while the guards passed. As soon as their footfalls had gone beyond earshot, she relaxed her hands and simply fell the rest of the way into the cart, hoping to the gods she had not made a mistake. The gods were good and she landed on her feet in the hay. With a sigh of relief, the princess ran to the stables.

As she rounded the corner of the wall she stopped and pressed her back against it; armed men were headed to the same place. If her suspicions were correct, none of the men could be trusted until her uncle was ousted from the throne. She took the bow from over her shoulder and nocked an arrow. As they passed her she overheard them saying something about killing a great beast and keeping a skull for the mantle. She knew what that meant, and she had to get to the stables before they did. They were on the direct path to the gate; she had to take the long route around the palace and past the carriage house. Sebele wasted no time. She returned the arrow to the quiver on her hip, shouldered her bow, and ran as fast as her still aching feet would take her.

She arrived at the rear door of the stable just as the armed men entered. They carried spears, war clubs, and axes, ready to unleash all manner of carnage. The lionesses, in their usual fashion were fast asleep; their bellies full of lamb and the bones of their meal strewn before them. There were more warriors than lionesses and if they were swift and quiet, then the men would dispatch the magnificent beasts before they would have time to resist. Sebele had to act. She swung the door open as they surrounded the first lion and raised their weapons.

"Eddel! Wake up! They are trying to kill you!" She was too late to save the first.

As the lionesses raised their drowsy heads and shook the slumber from their eyes, the first of her sleeping pride was slaughtered. The men stabbed, hacked, and battered the divine fire out of her body.

Eddel snarled at Sebele "Is this what you brought us here for?"

"Help me save them and I will explain after!" Sebele replied as she opened the pen gate and set Eddel loose upon the attackers. While a sleeping lioness is easy prey, one awakened and enraged was a different animal altogether.

Eddel threw herself at the company of assassins, and like her father Yihuda did to the hyenas, she tore them limb from limb. Sebele ran from pen to pen opening doors and releasing the lionesses, who joined the fray. In moments, the din of combat had ended, and Negus Iskander's men lay broken on the floor.

Eddel turned her attention to Sebele. "You had best tell me what just happened before I tear you to pieces and drink your blood like river water."

Sebele raised her hands. "Eddel, my uncle had my family killed, and he was going to kill me and you to cover up his crime. I did not bring you all here to be slaughtered."

"How can I believe you?" Eddel advanced on her, baring her teeth, her muzzle wet with blood.

"Because I came here to warn you instead of letting you die." Sebele stood her ground and arrow nocked in her bow. "Now you can come with me and we can seek our collective vengeance from this traitor, or you can try to kill me. I promise you, choose the latter, and you may succeed, but I will lay such a mark upon you that you will never forget that mistake."

Eddel stopped in her tracks and turned to look at the other lionesses; they stood quietly and watched the drama unfold. She returned her gaze to the princess. "Vengeance you say."

"Yes."

Eddel bowed her head. "Sit astride my back, and we will seek it together."

Without another word, Sebele jumped on to Eddel's back, and with the other lionesses behind them, they headed for the palace as fast as Eddel's four paws could carry them.

The commotion they drew in the stables roused the attention of the guard. When Sebele, Eddel, and the rest of the lionesses arrived at the palace gates, all of the armed men within earshot of the row in the stable were in front of the palace, their weapons at the ready. Lord Tadesse was among them.

"Princess Sebele, what is the meaning of this? Have you gone mad?" He asked.

"Mad? You ask me if I have gone mad? You seat a COWARDLY assassin on the throne and you have the audacity to ask me if I have gone mad?" Sebele snarled at him. "Send out my uncle that I may have words with him."

Lord Tadesse took a step forward and extended his hand. Eddel snarled at him, making the War Master reconsider his offer. "If your intention is to kill him, O Princess, we cannot oblige you. We must protect the crown."

Sebele scoffed. "Protect the crown, Lord Tadesse? Where were you to protect the crown when my father, my mother, my brothers, and my sisters were murdered in cold blood? Where were you to protect MY crown when I came to the city gates? If your loyalty to the crown was so pure, then you would turn your spears on the pretender that you call negus and uphold my claim!"

"Princess Sebele, be careful what you say!" First Minister Afewerek called from the balcony. "Such words are treason, and the price for such a sin against the crown is heavy."

"I have one question for you, First Minister Afewerek." Sebele fingered the arrow still nocked in her bow. "How did my family die?"

"What do you mean?" The minister forced a smile. "You know how they died, O Princess, you were there. Bandits killed them in the wild."

"You are a LIAR!" she shouted before she released her bowstring and sent an arrow to his chest. The First Minister, in shock from the sudden wound, lost his balance and tumbled over the railing, falling to his death at the feet of the royal guard.

"Arrest the princess!" Lord Tadesse ordered.

The lionesses roared.

"You will do no such thing." Sebele snarled. "I am Sebele bnit Yohannes, daughter of the Black Lion clan, wanderer of the Green Sea, favoured of the gods, and your rightful negast. You will not arrest me, you will not keep me from my right, and you will not keep me from my vengeance!"

"I said arrest her!" Lord Tadesse drew his sword and attacked.

Before his blow could land, Sebele loosed another arrow into his eye, killing him instantly. The palace guards lowered their spears and advanced. With a great roar, Eddel and the lionesses charged forward, swatting the spears aside with one paw and beating the men down with the other. The battle had begun.

Eddel had cleared a path into the palace. With Sebele on her back, she rushed into the great doors and began the hunt for Negus Iskander.

"ISKANDER!" Sebele shouted as she dismounted. "ISKANDER WHERE ARE YOU!?"

The answer came in the form of charging guards. Sebele loosed her arrows to distract them, and Eddel finished them with her fangs and claws. Shouldering her bow, Sebele pulled a sword from one of the corpses and squeezed the hilt in range.

"Throne room." She said to Eddel.

"Let us go find him." The lioness replied.

The pair stormed forth to the throne room, dispatching guards wherever they encountered them. The pair put them down so savagely that the rest of the guards turned and ran as Sebele and Eddel approached. Their path clear, it was not long before they reached the seat of power.

Princess Sebele kicked the ornately carved doors open and found her uncle sitting on the throne, a cup of wine in his hand and sullen look on his face.

"Sebele, my niece." He slurred, drunk from the contents of the overturned jug at his feet.

"Iskander, my uncle." Sebele's sword hand trembled with rage.

Negus Iskander took another sip from his cup. "I am so sorry. Negus Beka told me that I deserved to be king. I wanted it. I wanted the glory and the respect that came with this mantle. Negus Beka promised it to me in exchange for the death your father and his sons. I can make no children, and for the love of the gods I have tried. I wanted something that was mine. I would pass the throne to you when it was over, but I could not have the throne while Yohannes still lived. Even if Prince Negasi would take the throne after me, you would be his queen and our line would rule both Murhad and Mah. Since word returned, I have not slept a night. You asked me of my torn garment and shaken locks. The gods know how I wept for Yohannes and the rest of them. You were supposed to remain untouched. Your brothers may have been gone so that they could not challenge the crown, but Tigist and little Yezina would have marriages when they turned fifteen. All would be served. Now the only one served is me at the tip of this cup. The gods only know my sorrow, I do lament their deaths, and I lamented yours, O Sebele. I wept for you all. I will give you whatever you ask to soothe your aching heart."

"I want nothing from you." She snapped at him. "Your lamentations are meaningless to me. My heart no longer aches, it is empty."

Negus Iskander's eyes welled with drunken tears. "Be not so angry, my niece. Sunshaia will forgive me, if you can." He removed the crown from his head. "Here, I give you the crown. You may take it and mark yourself negast. I will order Sage Brehan to officiate the coronation."

Sebele lowered her blade. "No, I will not accept the crown as your gift of penance. Come hither uncle and we shall be at peace."

"What are you doing?" Eddel asked in confusion. Iskander opened his arms and stumbled toward his niece, his balance compromised by the amount of guilt he drank. Sebele stepped forward, her arms half extended.

"Thank you Sebele, thank you for your forgiveness." He wept. "I shall make all that I have done up to you, this I swear."

Sebele stepped back and looked her uncle in the eye. "I never said that you were forgiven." She grabbed his shoulder and thrust the blade deep into his belly. His eyes wide, Iskander gasped in disbelief.

Sebele twisted her weapon. "I said that we would be at peace, and I will not accept the crown as your gift. I will take it as my right."

Her uncle, still in shock from the thrust that ran him through, fell to his knees and then his side, shuddering as his life force drained from his body. Sebele took from him the blood soaked crown. She then withdrew the blade from his belly and hacked the head of her uncle from its shoulders. She needed proof that she had won. Before she carried the head out, she cut from it the locks that once hung down to her uncle's shoulders. She would not allow a coward the dignity of keeping them. With the same determination on her face that carried her through the crashing waves of the sea and the rolling green hills of Mah and Murhad, she raged to the nearest balcony, Eddel behind her.

When she stepped outside, the lionesses were still fighting the palace guards. One or two of the lionesses lay low, but many more of the guards did the same. She nodded to Eddel, who roared with the power of a victorious warrior, halting the hostilities.

Sebele held the crown in one hand and the bloody, severed head of her uncle in the other. "The pretender that you called negus is dead! Only this time his assassin had the wherewithal to look him in the eye when she ran him through!" Sebele casually tossed the head over the balcony for all below to see that it was in fact, the now late Negus Iskander. She then placed the crown upon her head. "Behold your right and truthful negast! I am the rightful ruler of Murhad! Follow me, and we will go to war and avenge my father, the negus so dishonourably slaughtered in a foreign land under the roof of a foreign ruler! Take your spears and point them south! Beat the drums of war, bring forth the elephants of bronze tusk, and we shall lay waste to their detestable city. Their crops will burn, their walls will crumble. We will not leave one lizard alive to climb in the rubble we leave behind in Mah!"

The men looked on her in silence, but none dared to raise his voice. "Will you come with me!?" Sebele raised her bloodied fist. "Will you come with me!?"

The lionesses roared their allegiance, for they knew her quality and would follow her anywhere into battle. The men looked at one another, still unsure of what to do. She killed the negus, and yet she was the rightful heir. Without the royal guard to endorse her, her hold on the throne would be tenuous at best. She needed their protection.

Sebele saw the conflict in their eyes and pressed her case further. "I am favoured by the gods. Did you not see that I emerged from the wilderness on the back of this great lioness? Here next to me is the living totem of my clan, of the sigil that YOU serve. Look on your shields, feel the bracelets on your wrists. You are of the Black Lions and here before you stands a black lioness. FOLLOW ME!"

"Hail Negast Sebele! Long live the negast!" The first voice broke the silence.

"Hail Negast Sebele!" Another voice shouted. "Let us march to war!"

More voices added to the chorus "Hail!"

Negast Sebele raised her hands as they cheered for her. "Bring Sage Brehan to consecrate my ascendance to the throne. Tomorrow there will be no feast in the palace. We will march on Mah, and we will see our spears drunk on the blood of our enemies!"

<u>Avenger</u>

Sebele looked over the rolling hills of the Green Sea. She watched as the many horned beasts of the great green hills ran, trotted, and bounded away from the rolling thunder that was her great army. Once her reign was consecrated, she immediately set about preparations for war. She called every man with a hand to carry a knife, sword, spear, hammer, club, or pitchfork to join her in avenging her family. Any lords, ministers, or soldiers that uttered even a word of doubt about her claim or the storm she was about to unleash had his head removed from his shoulders and mounted on a pike at the city gates. Captain Gebre was the first to die. She had him tortured, burning his feet and then rubbing them with salt. She had him flogged, and then broke his legs with a mallet. He died screaming. There was no room for detractors in Sebele's army. All who followed her in the march toward vengeance was either too loyal or too afraid to say even a word against her or her mission. Sebele led the procession of thirsty spear points from the back of Eddel, flanked by her lionesses.

Negast Sebele had her newly twisted locks wrapped into her war turban. Her skin of ebon was painted with ochre in swirling patterns of fire to honour Sunshadeen, who had given her the strength to rise to power. The bronze scales of her armour glittered in the light of Sun. In her hand she carried a bronze tipped spear, and in her saddlebags a bow and arrows. At her waist she carried a sword and dagger. On her feet she bore bronze toed war sandals. The young negast had armour fitted for Eddel and the lionesses: bronze caps to guard their heads, and scales to cover their throats and flanks.

Behind them marched great armoured war elephants with bronze blades fitted to their tusks and archers in baskets on their backs. Next there came the cavalry, men in crocodile hide armour carrying their shields and spears. They were followed by the royal guard, the regular infantry, and then whatever peasants could be pulled from the farms of Murhad. Today they would harvest blood from the Maheen.

Her arrival into Negus Beka's realm was announced by the first village her army burned. Save the fortunate soul they left alive with two severed hands to warn the next village, they slaughtered every man, woman, child, and animal before burning the settlement to ash. The heads of the chiefs of each village they burned on their path to Mah were mounted and carried next to the battle standards of her sea of spears. All of those heads were taken by Negast Sebele herself. She did not want to surprise Negus Beka with her arrival; she wanted to terrify him with it. She wanted to draw him out and face him on the field of battle. She wanted him to tremble with anger while his ministers begged him to sue for peace, though even if he offered his hand, she would cut it off and feed it to Eddel. There would be no mercy.

They encountered little resistance on the path to Mah. Small armed groups of men attempted to face them, and were either slaughtered or routed. Negast Sebele could only assume that they were trying to stall her advance while Negus Beka raised his army. As the wave of warriors washed over the final hills that stood between them and the city of Mah, Negast Sebele was greeted by men from her scouting party.

"Negast Sebele! Negast Sebele!" Their leader shouted as he rode forth. "The city of Mah is ahead of us, and Negus Beka has arrayed his army before the city. They await you."

"Good. Tell the drummers to beat their keberos and call the horns to blow. Announce that we are to prepare for battle."

"As you wish, O Negast." He bowed his head before riding off.

"Are you ready, Eddel? This will be far more fun than fighting hyenas." Sebele said to her lioness.

"I am ready. Lionesses, are you ready!?" Eddel growled.

The lionesses roared in affirmation. They were a terrifying sight with their shoulders the height of a fully grown man, teeth like daggers, and claws like short swords. Their armour glittered in the light of the gods against their midnight fur. They would guard the young queen on the field of battle as they did in the Green Sea and at the gates of the palace.

The pace of the drumbeats changed, and the warriors arranged themselves. The war elephants advanced to the front line, the infantry behind them, and the cavalry to the flanks. Sebele and her lionesses ran ahead to the top of the hill. Below her she saw the army of Negus Beka standing before the city. He had far more horsemen than she, but half the number of her war elephants. She could not properly count to compare the number of his infantry to her own. What she did know, was that she had brought more warriors, and there were no lions at his command.

She searched for Negus Beka's standard on the field. It was not among his warriors. She looked to the city walls. There he stood among his archers. She could barely make out his form, standing next to the noseless son she left him with before she cast herself into the sea. She swore to herself that by the end of this battle, Prince Negasi would be the first man in his family to lose his cock in a fight, and both he and his father would die screaming.

"May the gods have mercy on them, for I will not." She muttered under her breath.

Before she could return to the ranks of her army, a rider came forth under a banner of truce. She waited with her lionesses at the top of the hill and let them come.

"Sebele!" The well-dressed leader of the company of riders waved to her.

"That is Negast Sebele to you." She spat back. "Whatever terms you have for me, I am not interested."

He did not heed her. The messenger unrolled his papyrus scroll and gave her his master's demands. "All the same, Negus Beka demands that you take your army of savages and leave Mah. You will also repay him for the damage you have caused, for the villages you have burned, the livestock you have killed, and the people you have slaughtered."

Sebele turned the shaft of the spear in her grip. "And why does your negus not demand of me these things himself?"

The messenger smiled and returned the scroll to his saddlebag. "Because he doubts that you are honourable enough to respect a banner of truce."

Negast Sebele smirked. "Does he now? It seems that he is too much of a coward to look me in the eye."

The messenger looked her over and scoffed "Coward? Why would he fear you? You are just a wo-"

He never got the opportunity to finish speaking. Sebele drove the point of her spear through his throat, and with a motion of her free hand, bid the lionesses to tear the other riders from the backs of their horses and kill them as well.

"I am a negast." She said to him, as he feebly gripped at the spear, his eyes screaming in agony.

Sebele dismounted and stood over the fallen messenger. "I have a message for you to take back to your negus."

She drew her sword, removed his head and lifted his headless body back into the saddle of his horse. She rammed the flagpole into the herald's neck and sent his horse back to her enemies. She was not interested in peace. She wanted blood.

"There will be no quarter!" Sebele bellowed. She pulled herself into the saddle on Eddel's back and returned to the front line to order the advance. "Cut them down! Make them bleed! Follow me and grind them like ants beneath your heel! Let battle be joined!"

Drums pounded and horns blasted. Elephants trumpeted and the men clamoured for blood. Her army charged down the hill toward the vanguard of Mah, who stood with their spears at the ready. Their war elephants advanced to meet hers and with a great crash the giant beasts came together in a storm of bronze blades and arrows, accompanied by cries of blood fire and wails of death.

Sebele and her lionesses charged forth and met Negus Beka's elephants head on. Their bronze war tusks were no deterrent. Eddel raked her claws across the face of the first elephant she encountered. He responded with a thrust of his tusks under the direction of his mahout[23]. Sebele threw her spear at the driver but missed her target. Ducking a javelin lobbed in her direction, she took up her bow and loosed an arrow, striking him in the throat and sending the driver tumbling to the ground. Sensing that his driver had fallen, the elephant flew into a rage and savagely charged at Sebele and Eddel. Without hesitation, Eddel leapt past the elephant's tusks and onto his back, cutting through the archers she found there. The lioness then pulled the elephant down and clamped her jaws around his throat, tearing through the flesh and ending his life. Sebele continued to shoot her arrows as the targets came.

Arrows flew in all directions, striking warriors down with no discrimination. Horses and elephants wailed as they were shot and stabbed. Men screamed and cut one another to pieces. Spears broke, shields split, and skulls cracked. The bodies began to pile, and the broken corpses of fallen warriors served as the grim building blocks for a wall of their own. Sebele soon found herself on foot, standing on the growing pile of the dead and dying men, pressing the point of her bronze blade into the chest of an adversary. Her footing was difficult to hold as the armour and skin of the corpses beneath her had become slick with blood and bile.

A pair of strong hands grabbed her by the collar of her cuirass from behind and pulled her down. She slid down the pile of corpses

---

[23] Elephant Driver

and found herself laying in the blood and entrails of a disemboweled horse. Before she could regain her footing, she spied a war club heading for her face. She parried the strike with her sword. It bent from the force of the blow but protected her from injury. The weapon came down again; she blocked it with her bent blade. She drew the dagger from her waist and drove it into the ankle of her attacker, costing him his footing. No sooner did he tumble to the ground did she climb on top of him and end his life by driving her dagger into his throat.

She rose to her feet and took up his war club. Her veins were hot with fire. Her war turban had come loose during her fall. She tore it from her head and set her locks free. They danced in the winds of war as she scanned the battlefield.

"TO ME!" She waved the war club over her head. "TO ME!"

Every one of her men within earshot rallied to her, as did her lionesses. She mounted Eddel's back and rode to the top of the writhing pile of death.

"We are winning." Eddel declared.

"We are winning out here, but our target is in there." Negast Sebele pointed to the city.

A horn blasted from the city walls, and Negus Beka's men soon disengaged and ran to the city gate, which had opened just enough to allow them to enter.

"THEY ARE RETREATING! DO NOT LET THEM CLOSE THE GATE!" Negast Sebele screamed at her men. "SEND THE ELEPHANTS!"

What elephants remained charged at the slightly ajar city gate to batter it open. They were met with a hail of arrows, javelins and stones, some bouncing off of their armour, others hitting their mark and killing the archers in the baskets or the mahouts on the elephants' necks. One managed to reach the gate just as they were pressing it closed. The pachyderm lowered his head and with a great thrust, pushed back the men that sought to block their entry and swung one of the doors wide open. Sebele and her men wasted no time. The elephants stormed in, goring all in their path before Sebele rode past the curtain of arrows and entered the city gates.

"Let the slaughter begin!" She shouted. "Burn them all! Burn everything! RAZE MAH TO THE GROUND!"

The gods were kind to Sebele. She watched in savage delight as her army flooded the streets of Mah. Cooking fires were now house fires. Songs were screams, and every alley and market square was filled with sounds of swords crossing and men dying. Mah would be destroyed, but Sebele's revenge was not complete.

"Eddel, we must find Negus Beka and his family." Sebele snarled. "My justice awaits."

Through the carnage that had overtaken the seaside city of her quarry, Sebele, Eddel, and the lionesses charged toward the palace compound at the city centre. They cut their way through the soldiers, militia, and any citizen brave enough to raise even a finger against Sebele's advance. She would not be stopped. They arrived at the gates to the compound and were met with arrows from between the crenellations. More lionesses fell. They took refuge behind the houses and regrouped.

"I will not be stopped now." Sebele raged.

"You will be stopped if their arrows kill us." Eddel replied. "Look up."

"What do you mean?" Sebele was confused.

"These houses are not far from the walls. I can jump from that rooftop over the wall."

"And the arrows?"

"You have given us bronze coats. If a pack of hyenas did not end us, then these wretches have no hope."

Sebele nodded. "Then let us go."

As quickly as any cat could climb, the lionesses took to the rooftops and bounded across them, zipping from left to right until they approached the wall and launched themselves into the air. Sebele held on to Eddel's saddle as tightly as she could and prayed to the gods that this was the right decision. The landing was not as smooth as she hoped. Eddel hit the ground with a thud, and Sebele was thrown from the saddle. Sebele rose to her feet and was immediately set upon by Negus Beka's royal guard.

She charged at the nearest man. She swat his spear point aside with her free hand and struck him on the crown of his head with the war club before he could raise his shield to protect himself. The blow dented his helmet and dazed him long enough for her to strip it from him and strike a finishing blow. Two more spear points came for her. She took up the fallen guard's shield and covered her advance. She checked one of the guards with her shield arm and struck the other on the head before turning to strike the first again. She hit them, one then the other, protecting herself from blows with the shield until they fell at her feet. Sebele dropped the war club and pulled a sword from one of their belts. She charged into the fray with the lionesses as they dispatched the archers on the wall. Before long, all of their enemies were dead.

Sebele roared in triumph along with her lionesses, shaking her locks as she held her blood soaked weapons aloft.

"Eddel! Eddel!" Sebele called out to her companion. "Let us go and seek out Beka and his brood. There is yet death for us to deal."

There was no answer. Sebele searched the courtyard for Eddel, for she could not hear the voice of the brave lioness in her head. She turned, turned, and turned again, and then she discovered the cause of Eddel's silence. She lay on her side, a javelin planted in her belly. It had caught her in the jump under the hem of her armour. The pain was too great for the lioness to remove it on her own, though not for want of trying.

"Eddel!" Sebele ran to her companion's side. "Eddel, speak to me, I cannot hear you!"

The lioness looked up at her, and then looked at the javelin. Sebele nodded and dropped her weapons. She gripped the javelin and looked into Eddel's eyes again."

"Yes." The lioness' feeble voice whispered in her head.

With a great heave, Sebele pulled the weapon from Eddel's belly. The lioness yelped in pain, and then lay her head down again.

"You should open that gate and let your men in. More Maheen will come." Eddel said.

Sebele nodded and ran to the gate. With the help of one of the other lionesses, she lifted the wooden beam away from the doors and dropped it on the ground with a great thud. She pushed the door open, then turned her face to the palace.

"My prize awaits me inside the palace." Sebele wiped the sweat from her brow.

"Then go and claim it, though I cannot follow you." Eddel replied.

Sebele walked over to her fallen companion and kissed her between the eyes. "You are always with me."

She stood up and took into her possession the javelin, sword, and shield she had acquired from the fallen guards. These would be the tools of her vengeance.

"Those who would follow, come!" She called to the lionesses; they followed her out of the light and into the shadow of the palace.

"BEKA! NEGASI!" She shouted, her voice echoing through the hallways. "BEKAAAA! NEGASIIIII!"

Room by room, she stormed through the palace and found nothing. With every empty room she found behind a closed door, her rage only increased. They would not escape; they would not rob her of her vengeance.

"BEKA! NEGASI!" Sebele shouted as she paced back and forth. "Can none of you smell them? Are they here?"

The lionesses sniffed the air, searching for a hint of their leader's quarry.

"Over there." One of their voices echoed in Sebele's head.

Negast Sebele looked at the great doors to the throne room. Someone was hiding behind that door. Without a second thought, she stomped over to the doors and kicked them open. "BEKA! NEGASI!"

The response was an arrow that narrowly missed Sebele's head. More arrows came, and Sebele ducked under her shield, eyes searching wildly for archers. They were in the gallery.

"CHARGE!" She shouted as she surged forward towards the nearest staircase, arrows thrumming into the wicker and hide shield she held above her head. Too full of arrows to be useful, she cast the shield aside and ran up the stairs with her javelin in hand. She did not count the number of steps she took, but soon enough she and the lionesses had reached the gallery and were immediately set upon by Negus Beka's royal guard.

"All glory to Sunshadeen!" Negast Sebele bellowed as she ran toward her foes.

She threw the javelin at the nearest man to her; the force of the throw sent it halfway through his rawhide shield and nearly into his face. She did not allow him to recover. By the time he had dropped his shield; she had grabbed the shaft of his spear and thrust her sword into his throat. More men charged forward, and they were met with the wrath of her lionesses. Spears broke against the force of their massive claws, and where they were covered with armour was proof against the blades. The archers had more luck, catching a leg or exposed flank with their arrows. This would not save them. At the head of her lioness, Sebele cut them down. She slashed, hacked, and threw them over the railing, sending them to their deaths on the limestone below. The last of them tried to escape, but Sebele would see his flight denied.

"Hold him!" she ordered one of the lionesses, who caught him by the leg before he reached the staircase.

The lioness turned him on his back and put a massive paw on his chest, holding him in place.

Sebele squatted near him, the skirt of her scale coat draped over her knees. "I am only going to ask you this once. Where is the royal family?"

"I-I-I" A puddle of urine spread on the floor between his legs.

"I am going to count to three, and if you do not tell me I am going to let this lioness tear your stupid head from your stupid shoulders with her teeth." Sebele tapped him on the cheek. "One, two –"

"In the dining hall!" he shouted. "The royal family is in the dining hall. Prince Negasi guards them with the rest of the royal guard. Now please let me live!"

"When did I say I was going to let you live? I only said that this lioness was not going to eat you." Sebele smirked before slashing his throat with her sword.

Negus Beka hid like a coward with his wife and children in the dining hall, the very same hall where she drank coffee with her family for the last time. This was the very same place where Negus Beka made his false declarations of respect and friendship. Soon his screams of pain would dance in the air instead of the aroma of coffee. Sebele took up another spear and shield. With fire burning in her viens, she marched with her lionesses to the dining hall.

"I see you came back for me my betrothed." The voice of that yam-headed prince made Sebele's skin crawl. "You should have drowned in the sea!"

There he stood, armoured and armed in a shield wall formation with his royal bodyguards. He wore a false nose to cover the wound she inflicted on him before she threw herself into the sea. He held a javelin in one hand and a shield in the other, his head protected by a bronze cap and turban.

"The gods have sent me to finish what I started on your face!" Sebele snarled.

"I see you are as savage as ever." Prince Negasi spat back. "If it is any consolation, your baby sister, Yezina was it? She barely cried when I choked the life out of her tiny body, the same way I am going to do to you. When this fight is over, I am going to choke you and fuck you raw, dead or alive."

"Do you remember what I told you the last time you threatened me?" Sebele turned the spear in her hand. "Perhaps I should show you."

She charged forward, throwing the spear at Prince Negasi. He raised his shield to protect his head and swatted the weapon aside. Sebele and her lionesses rushed the formation, her sword held aloft and shield out before her.

Prince Negasi and his men held their ground, driving the lionesses back with the points of their spears. The odd javelin would fly from somewhere in the packed formation. Most missed their mark; others glanced off of the lioness' armour. The fight continued in this way for an untold amount of time. Sebele and the lionesses would attack, but then would be driven back by the tight formation and long spears. Weariness from an entire day on the battlefield began to take its toll, and each of Sebele's attempts to break the battle line grew feebler than the one that preceded it. The lionesses were exhausted, and Prince Negasi and his guard outnumbered them.

The prince saw them beginning to tire and decided to take advantage. "Advance!"

He and his men marched forward, their shields interlocked and their spear points forward. Sebele watched the wall of bronze, wood, and hide approach as she knelt, sweat running the patterns of war paint on her face as she panted. She forced herself to her feet despite the weakness in her legs and the heaviness of her arms. She raised her shield and squeezed the hilt of her sword.

"Lionesses! We have come this far! Do not let them turn us back!" She bellowed. "All glory to Sunshadeen!"

The lionesses, also panting from exhaustion, roared and followed the princess in the attack. They clashed with Prince Negasi and his men, batting the spears aside and fighting to pull the shields from the arms of the men that bore them. The lionesses began to fall before the spears, even as Sebele pushed forward and felled one man after the other, it was not enough. Prince Negasi and his men still pressed forward, driving Sebele and her lionesses back towards the wall.

"Leave the bitch alive!" Shouted Prince Negasi as another lioness fell to a series of spear thrusts. "I want to know how much tighter her hole is than her mother's!"

The tip of a spear cut into the flesh of her cheek, causing blood to run down her face and neck. She did not see who the spear belonged to, so she forced her sword point past the top of the nearest shield and into the eyes of the man that held it, blinding him. This was still not enough. Sebele could not believe that she was losing this battle. After all she had done, all that she had survived, the gods would abandon her like this. The gods would not carry her on the waves of the endless waters, guard her against the dangers of the wilderness, give her such ferocious protectors, and the crown of Murhad only to bring her back to Mah and have her die by the hand of that disfigured monster.

More lionesses died, and those that remained with Sebele were backed into a corner. She gritted her teeth and thought of the wild dogs that chased her. If she was going to die, she was going to be sure that Prince Negasi and his men earned every drop of blood they spilled. She looked to her left and her right, and saw her lionesses, bloodied and snarling, ready to give their last with her.

Sebele raised the sword over her head, and just as she was about to unleash what she thought was her final war cry, Sunshadeen again showed his favour. Up the stairs came Eddel, running at the head of the royal guard of Murhad.

"PROTECT THE NEGAST!" shouted their captain, pointing to her with his spear.

Eddel roared, and along with Sebele's royal guard she crashed into the back of Prince Ncgasi's formation like the head of an enraged bull elephant, cutting them down sooner than they could turn and fight. Sebele felt renewed strength, and with a great shout of blood fire she charged again, casting her foes to the ground and grinding them beneath her heel. Before long, Prince Negasi and the handful of men that remained were surrounded.

"Leave the noseless freak alive!" She shouted. "He belongs to me!"

In moments, all of Prince Negasi's men were dead, and he was all that was left. Sebele's men dragged the prince and dropped him at her feet, battered and disarmed. Negast Sebele looked down on him, humbled beneath her.

"You have me now, bitch. Kill me and be done with it." He spat at her past his bloodied lips.

"That is Negast Bitch to you." Sebele kicked his abdomen. "Say it."

"Say what?"

"Say Negast Bitch."

"No."

"SAY IT!" Sebele kicked him again.

Negasi coughed, blood draining from his mouth. "Negast Bitch. You are mad."

"You haven't the slightest idea." She tore the false nose from his face. "You look better like this. Hold him."

Prince Negasi was confused. "Wait what are you doing?"

"I asked you if you remember what you said to me that night I jumped out of the window." Sebele drew a dagger from the belt of one of her guards. "Do you remember? Spread his legs."

"What are you talking about?" The prince's expression changed from defiant to terrified, this was the first time she looked at him and felt like smiling.

She lifted his kilt and cut the front of his trousers. "You offered me something, and now I have come to take what is mine."

The horror of what was about to happen set in. "No, please, no!" Negassi began to buck and kick, swivelling his hips to safeguard his manhood from her grasp. Resistance was futile.

Sebele grabbed Prince Negasi's cock. "Yes." She began to saw at it with the dagger, taking her time and relishing the moment.

Prince Negasi screamed in agony and bucked as much as the five men that restrained him would allow. No amount of pleading and screaming would be enough to purchase clemency; rather, it only encouraged her to take her time. Sebele purposefully drew the dagger in long strokes against his manhood as she cut it away. Eventually the pain and blood loss caused the newly made eunuch to lose consciousness.

"Wake him up." Sebele ordered her men. "Slap and shake him if you have to, but wake him up."

Her men did as they were told, slapping and shaking Prince Negasi until he opened his eyes. He looked as though he had awakened from a nightmare, only to realize that the nightmare was real, and it had not yet ended. Sebele dangled Negasi's severed cock in front of his face.

"Not as big as you made it seem." She smirked. "At least you saved me the disappointment on our wedding night. Now strip him, my lionesses are hungry."

She turned her attention to the doors to the dining hall as her men stripped Prince Negasi of his armour. They threw him naked, bleeding and shivering before the lionesses, who wasted no time filling their bellies with this flesh. He died screaming.

"Open the door." Sebele commanded.

Her men pulled the mahogany doors apart and Sebele entered. The room was eerily quiet. She scanned the room for a sight of Negus Beka. There was no one sitting at the tables, and no one on the dais. Suddenly, the sound of a metal goblet scraping against the stone floor caught her attention. It came from the far corner of the room behind one of the tables. She ran over to the source of the sound and found the entire royal family dead on the floor, save Negus Beka. He looked at her, smiled and raised the goblet to his lips.

"NO!" She shouted as she ran forward and slapped it from his hand. "You will not rob me of my justice!"

The goblet clanged as it hit the floor, spilling red wine in all directions. Sebele grabbed Negus Beka by the collar and dragged him to the middle of the hall.

"Kneel." She snarled, pointing to the floor.

"To you? Never! I will not give you the satisfaction." Negus Beka stood defiant.

"Animals like you should know when they are conquered." Sebele pointed to his knees.

A pair of her guards struck Negus Beka behind his legs with their war clubs. His knees buckled and he fell prostrate before her. He looked up at her with the foulest expression that he could muster. Sebele smiled back and dropped Prince Negasi's cock before him.

"I have ended your line." She said. "Your family is fortunate that you were generous enough to poison them before I found you."

"What do you intend to do with me?" Negus Beka failed at resisting the urge to tremble.

"You shall receive the fate due to all men that murder women and children in their beds, that rob daughters of their fathers with false promises of an alliance, the same fate as men that turn brothers against each other and tear families apart." She wiped the blood from Negasi's cock off of her hand and on to Negus Beka's sweaty cheek. "You have destroyed my world, and now I will destroy yours. Captain."

"Yes, O Negast." A warrior stepped forward.

Negast Sebele put a hand on the captain's shoulder. "Have a cross built on the nearest hill to the city. Have Negus Beka stripped and waiting there for me. Be sure to have extra nails for me. Negus Beka is going to see his city torn apart, brick by brick. Every house is to be burned. Every man, woman, and child is to be put to the sword. I do not want to see the tiniest lizard left alive in this city. Once you have smashed every stone, cut down every tree, and burned every scrap of papyrus, the land is to be salted. I do not want a single weed to grow from the ashes of Mah. This will be a dead city, and a reminder to all of those that would insult the gods with false blessings. It will be a lesson to those that would have the audacity to think that they could strike against the Black Lion clan and live to celebrate it." She made eye contact with Beka "You, Negus Beka, will die screaming like your son; only your death will not be so merciful. Captain, take him."

"You will pay for this!" Shouted Negus Beka as they bound his hands and dragged him away. "You will pay for this, you bitch! The Sunbaka take you!"

"I have already paid." She said under her breath as the room cleared.

The captain's voice faded into the distance as she heard him order the men to sweep the palace for survivors and begin the demolition of Mah. Once everyone had gone out of earshot, Sebele fell to her knees and wept. She cupped her face with her hands, and she wept.

"Thank you." She whispered to the gods. "Thank you for my justice."

Sebele could not tell if she wept for her lost family, the betrayal from her uncle, for the victory over her foes, or the fact that she somehow survived all of this. Whatever the reason, she let the symphony of emotions pour out through her tears.

Sebele felt a large, furry head press against her. "Why do you weep, O Sebele? You have won. Your honour is restored and your enemies are vanquished."

"My Eddel!" Negast Sebele wrapped her arms around the lioness' neck. "I thought you lost, I thought that javelin had finished you."

"I am wounded, but not dead." Eddel replied. "Soon, I will be gone."

"What do you mean?" Sebele wiped the tears from her eyes and looked the majestic beast in the eye.

Eddel's gaze was distant, longing for the Green Sea and its dancing grasses. Though she was glorious in her armour, Sebele knew that this was not where the lioness belonged. The wilderness was her home, and she had to return to it.

"You know where I belong." The lioness replied. "The rolling green hills call me. The wild game runs free, and there are no stone walls or stables to keep me. I belong in the wilderness among my kind, as do the lionesses."

"Stay with me, Eddel." Sebele pleaded. "I am negast now; there is none that would dare touch a whisker on your face without fear of death. Do not leave me, we have seen too much now."

"I will visit you, O Sebele, but the time has come for us to go." Eddel nuzzled Sebele. "You will see me again."

Sebele wiped away the last of her tears and rose to her feet. "At least allow me to strip the armour from you before you go."

The lioness presented her flank, and Sebele unbuckled the bronze cap and scale coat, letting them drop to the floor. Sebele did the same for the other lionesses as well. One by one, they each nuzzled her affectionately before making their way out of the city and back into the wild.

Sebele, once she gathered herself, made her way to the hill where Negus Beka awaited her under guard. She nailed him to the cross and hung him there for three days, forcing him to watch Mah be reduced to rubble while birds of carrion picked at his flesh. As she had commanded, every stone tablet was broken and every scroll of papyrus burnt. Every man, woman, and child unable to escape was put to the sword.

Every animal, domestic and wild, within the walls of the city was slaughtered, and the land was covered in salt to kill any chance of life re-establishing itself under or within the walls of Mah. When the destruction of the city was complete, Sebele had Negus Beka, half dead and covered in puss-filled sores, boiled to death in a large pot of coffee before throwing his corpse into the sea. He did not deserve the dignity of being burned on a pyre. The debt was paid.

<u>Epilogue</u>

"Abbu, did Eddel come back?" Princess Gete asked, her large eyes now drooping with drowsiness.

I smiled at her. "That she did, but after many monsoons. When she did return, her belly was full of cubs. She bore them in the stables of Murhad, the same ones where our lions sleep tonight. Since then, they were our loyal companions in times of peace and our greatest comrades in times of war."

"Will I ever have a lion?" Gete yawned.

"You cannot possess a lion my dear. They are with you, they are never yours." I kissed her forehead and rose to my feet. "I have given you your story, now you have to go to sleep."

She did not answer. Sleep had taken her before I finished speaking.

"Well I did not think the story was that boring." I winked at my wife.

She extended her graceful arm and beckoned me. "I am sure your speech at the wedding feast will capture everyone's attention. Now come, Dejen, I am sure the guests are anxious for the ceremony. It usually never takes this long to begin."

"As I said, my dear." I linked her arm with mine. "I am the negus and you are the negast. They can wait until we arrive."

We strolled to the great hall surrounded by our guards. Tonight was a great night. All seven of our sons were to be married. Through years of trade deals, gifts, negotiations, and half of the sheep and cattle of Murhadin, I was finally able to arrange their marriages to the daughters of the seven greatest neguseen and warlords of the Horn. Through I could not secure the hand of the first daughter of every clan; one was enough to broker peace. After all, I could not expect them to accept the marriage of their first daughter to even my second son. That would be an insult. They did, however, agree to take part in the greatest wedding feast ever seen in our lands. They came from every corner, Khadra, Broken Spear, Hajid Island, High Stone, Black Mane, the trade hub of Munxa, and even New Mah. Their kin followed them. Not one member of their clans would dare to miss this. They brought their captains and their guards, their ministers and their sages. Some even saw fit to bring their nameless sons and daughters. My hall was the centre of the centre of all of the greatest families to grace the green hills of the Horn.

Gifts had come to our city gates from every corner of the Sunya. Scrolls were gifted to us from the kings of Waha, swift horses from the rulers of Basgin and Resjur, precious stones hewn from Limestone's mountain ranges. The distant city of Dimuk sent ships filled with the most fragrant cedar from their forests. Even the Rahisheen clans sent exotic textiles and bronze sculptures from the distant lands they travelled. The coffers of my sons and their new wives would overflow with bounty, the heart's desire of any parent.

Tsion's arm was trembling with anxiety. Many of these families had met us on the battlefield. All had brought death to some number of our kin. Her nervousness was not unexpected. She knew the importance of this night to the stability of our region.

We arrived at the hall, and the doors were opened to us. The air was full of the mingling scents of frankincense, stewed meat, and greens. The steam from the platters and pots danced to the rhythm of clapping hands and wailing masenqo, played by my eldest daughter Yezina as she sang the anthem of our clan:

> *We fear no foe, evermore we hold our blades,*
> *We are people of the hills and plains,*
> *Surrender in battle is an enduring stain,*
> *We bring honour to our fathers' names,*

"We present to you all, Negus Dejen and Negast Tsion of the Black Lion clan!" Balambra Abune announced our arrival.

We were greeted with cheers and lifted cups of wine. I raised my arms and cheered with the crowd. Tsion smiled demurely, as she always did when she felt on edge. I reassured her with a kiss on the palm, and our hands held high, we danced and sang up the centre aisle to the seats that awaited us at the head table on the dais.

Dancing girls took to the centre aisle and continued to delight the room as their shoulders bounced while they tossed their proud afros from side to side. As my wife and I took our seats, she looked at me, her eyes asking me if this was the right thing for us to do. I smiled at her and nodded. Tonight would be the last night of war in the Horn, and the first night of peace for a thousand generations. My eyes met with Captain Yekob, who motioned to his men to bar every door in the room. I scanned the great hall, looking to my nephews and my nieces, to my brothers and my cousins. They all nodded to me and smiled, pouring extra cups of wine for our guests and encouraging the merrymaking.

My sons had already gone to consummate their newly made unions, as was our way. After the ceremony, they would complete their union under the eyes of three witnesses. When the first entwining of their bodies was complete, the pair would be left to enjoy themselves, and then would dance for their families at the climax of the celebration feast. If those young grooms were anything like their father, they would need considerable time before coming to dance for their kin. My wife nodded to me that she was ready, and I rose to my feet, cup in hand and a broad smile on my face.

The music stopped as I prepared to give my speech. "Here in this room, we, the people of the Horn become kin to each other. We put down our spears and raise our cups to everlasting peace!"

The guests cheered.

"I must apologise for taking so long for the coffee ceremony tonight. I know that the wedding ceremony was delayed a little, but one bride is difficult enough to prepare. You can imagine seven!"

The guests laughed and raised their cups, some yelling out "Amnaeen[24]" as though a great sage had spoken.

"Now, I again must thank you all for coming. I know the journey has been long, and not all of you could have made it here, but to those of you that have, thank you. Hail to the Bush Pig clan, the Pata Monkey clan, the Grey Panyas, the Green Mambas, the Wild Cat clan, and last but never least, the Sun Squirrel clan!"

I held my cup forward. "May not another drop of blood be shed in anger between us after this night."

I put the cup to my lips, and all in attendance did the same. I finished my water and dropped the bronze cup at my feet, the signal for the main event to begin. In an instant, my kin and I fell upon our guests, shotels drawn from beneath our tables and knives from our waistbands. The other clans were too drunk or surprised to retaliate. Our blades cut them to pieces like the claws of our namesake. Some managed to resist, but they were promptly laid low by a blade they did not see. Their escorts that waited outside of the palace would be too drunk or asleep in the arms of whores sent to distract them. Those that would not surrender and pledge allegiance to the supreme

---

[24] An exclamation denoting affirmation, usually in a spiritual context, an evocation of the blessed divine

rule of the Black Lion clan would be put to the sword. With the neguseen of the other six royal clans and their immediate heirs gone, my sons would rule their lands and their clans as their lawful chiefs, and I would be their king. The Horn would be unified after this final night of slaughter. The limestone floor was wet and red, as though a hundred pots of wine had broken and their contents were left to run rivers beneath our feet.

As I brought my shotel to bear upon Negus Habash of the Pata Monkey clan, he asked me "why?" He would never understand. I wanted peace. I wanted stability. So long as more than one man could wear a crown in the Horn, there would never be peace among us. There would never be peace for the children of our lands. For the sake of the feisty little girl I left sleeping, I would personally cut the heads from the shoulders of a thousand times a thousand chiefs to know that she would not grow up to suffer the pains of Negast Sebele.

SONGS OF THE SUNYA

Tales from the Sands of Time Volume I

<u>Old Sunsha to English Glossary</u>

1) *Salayem na sulayamneen fitayat anuneen* - Peace and blessings be upon (all of) you
2) *Chicheu* - Panther
3) *Ra* - The power of an amplified divine fire
4) *Anu p'at wahdit baq yalla karera laimar! Tag zahit bnit Bhagir dakera!* - You will not take another step! This child is a daughter of Bhagir!
5) *Y'arit* - Chief
6) *Khurt* - A tall stork with a bill so large that it sometimes falls over when it bends down to drink
7) *Udrahdu* - Wise Elder
8) *Dulit* - Women with the special skill of aiding in childbirth
9) *Mazkhee* - Also known as "turned ones", people who drink the blood of the Dzinee and become misshapen creatures that thirst for human blood
10) *Dzinee* - Creatures created during the time of Ama, the first Red Cloak as protectors of the weak, they were born of the corruption of nature and now serve the Dark Sages
11) *Barkudzin* - A class of Dzinee, creatures created from the corruption of nature in the name of war
12) *Abbu* - Father
13) *Fut* - Down
14) *Fit* - Up
15) *Kibokeen* – Hippopotami
16) *Yallanu, dzutnu duaratou* - Go, bring my chair
17) *Naim, O Yashnusunabra* - Yes O Great Sage

18) *Negus* - King
19) *Ama* - Mother
20) *Dabo* - Bread
21) *Negast* - Queen
22) *Yaheen* - Humans/Mankind
23) *Mahout* - Elephant Driver
24) *Amnaeen* - An exclamation denoting affirmation, usually in a spiritual context, an evocation of the blessed divine.